After the Stranger

IMAGINARY DIALOGUES WITH CAMUS

After
the Stranger

Imaginary Dialogues with Camus

By HAYDEN CARRUTH

ᴸᵁᴸᵁᴸᵁᴸᵁᴸᵁᴸᵁᴸᵁᴸᵁᴸᵁᴸᵁᴸᵁᴸᵁᴸᵁᴸᵁ

Alas, thoughte I, what aventures
Han these sory creatures,
That they amonges al the pres,
Shulde thus be shamed gilteles!
But what! hit moste nedes be.

THE MACMILLAN COMPANY, NEW YORK
COLLIER-MACMILLAN LIMITED, LONDON

DESIGNED BY RONALD FARBER

Acknowledgment is made to the following for permission
to use copyrighted materials:

Alfred A. Knopf, Inc., for quotations from

The Stranger by Albert Camus,
translated by Stuart Gilbert, copyright
1946 by Alfred A. Knopf, Inc.

The Rebel by Albert Camus,
translated by Anthony Bower, copyright
1954 by Alfred A. Knopf, Inc.

Resistance, Rebellion and Death by Albert Camus,
translated by Justin O'Brien, copyright ©
1960 by Alfred A. Knopf, Inc.

George Braziller, Inc., for a quotation from

Saint Genet: Actor and Martyr by Jean-Paul Sartre,
translated by Bernard Frechtman, copyright ©
1963 by George Braziller, Inc.

To Martha

part one

_⅃⅂⅃⅂⅃⅂⅁_

IN THE House of the Fishes, which is to say in March, the weather is damp and often windy. A person visiting there may feel extremely uncomfortable, and disturbed in mind as well; for his discomfort will be in no wise lessened, and may even be increased, by his knowledge that the moist wind is antecedent to rebirth in the coming spring. For example, such a person may find himself after dark, at ten o'clock of the evening, in a side street of a suburban town. Black remnants of snow encrust the curbs and gutters. The wind agitates the darkness violently; the streetlights glimmer palely and seem more remote than usual. Moreover, gusts of rain batter him with a spasmodic force which he cannot interpret as other than vicious and vengeful, although he loathes the sentimentality which attributes feelings to the works of nature. Worst of all is the darkness and windiness in the region of his heart.

The person is walking beside a wall. The wall, which rises to eye-level, is composed of cobbles, uniform in size and neatly mortared; it encloses the elevated grounds of a suburban home, although nothing is visible from the street but a grove of mature spruce and pine. The trees are dark, a dense composition of shadow and wind-moan. Across the street smaller homes crouch on their squares of lawn, open to view but now dark, with only a glinting reflection of the streetlight here and there, on windows and brass door fixtures. A black convertible, with the top raised, is parked at the curb, directly across the street, and a man and a woman are about to enter it. They pause a moment beneath the streetlight: the woman not young but quite beautiful nevertheless, dressed for evening, a raincoat flung carelessly over her shoulders, revealing a white gown and white gloves, a glitter of jewelry; the man darkly clad, standing beyond the streetlight's pale cone. The woman raises her hand, and laughs; the laughter, in the strange night, is delicately clear and beautiful, like a bird's song. At this moment the wind hurls its fiercest blow, a buffeting, explosive force that assails the pines and spruces with a roar not heard since childhood.

The person totters, and then turns, fleeing awkwardly in the direction from which he has come.

⌐⌐⌐⌐⌐

[Dear diary, my stomach is coming up, you are as revolting as ever. Never doubt it! But say, seriously, wouldn't you think a man of parts might enjoy a more profitable companion? Turning to you, pleading with you, each time the demon strikes: what degradation. You, no more than a scrap of wind from my own belly.

He struck tonight, though, without a question; the heaviest blow in a long time. A most demoniac demon. Which is nonsense, of course. Yet the notion has a certain power, a certain rightness, which is more than can be said for anything the doctors have invented. First, because the "attack" is unmistakably within; sometimes, during the worst of it, I feel as if my insides were enormously enlarged, turned into a cavern, full of echoes and air currents springing from hidden sources. Second, because, at the same time, the agent of "attack," the torturer, the assailant, the *Gauleiter*, seems so completely other than oneself, not only uncontrollable but unknowable. Inside but other: what can it be but the demon? When that fellow came to the Gadarene country, he met a man with an unclean spirit who dwelt among the tombs and always, "night and day," was crying and cutting himself with stones; the fellow said simply, "Come out of the man, thou unclean spirit." Whereupon the man was well and sane. (However, his name was Legion.) Not altogether nonsense, then. For in terms of desire and need a thing may be impossible without being incomprehensible.

Christ, Christ, is it any more possible for being comprehended? You religious guys are the dreamers. And painters? The junkmen of the soul.

Well, the scene was imaginable enough: wall, streetlight, wind and rain, the apparition of a laughing woman. At that moment, when the laugh tinkled so brilliantly in the roaring wind, then madness struck. For the thousandth time. Incidentally, the woman was no apparition, but quite real, I have seen her before, I think, the one with the old-fashioned-looking brunette bob who promenades occasionally in the morning; she resembles the women in the Lucky Strike ads from *Vanity Fair*. Not tonight, however; she was beautiful. A telling gesture: her gloved hand upraised gracefully, light against dark, at the moment when her glass-like laughter broke into the tumult of the wind. And I want to scotch at its inception the idea that she was a fantasy, all the more since the vision of her was, although caught (photographed by my mind) in the fullness of reality, composed of the elements which ordinarily do make up hallucination: extreme contrast, perfect simplicity, a concentration of unspoken meanings. If the suggestion of hallucination were to enter my memory of this vision, a memory which is of the order that remains until death, it would be a permanent and ineradicable contamination. But the "suggestion of hallucination" has already entered my memory! Blast it, I myself opened the door to it simply by considering the possibility; and this, this consideration, was unwilled and unwanted, an inevitable link in the chain of mental events running back to God knows when, a determinative priority. You see, you see how the demon works? The contamination has occurred. And what quantities of energy and anguish I must now expend in the ensuing years to discriminate the woman from the possible illusion of the woman!

Easy enough, in any event, to preconstruct the doctors' interpretation, having been well schooled! Simple case of anxiety hysteria, resulting from anger directed toward the woman (for her beauty and freedom) and augmented to the point of uncontrollable panic by the sympathetic violence of the wind in the fir trees. (Will I never hear the wind stir again without that surge of terror?) I don't say it's wrong. On the contrary, it must be right, because only a psychomechanical malfunction could produce so excessive a response, like a calculating machine gone out of order and whizzing in uncontrollable multiplications. Yet the notion is unsatisfactory in terms of usefulness, not at all the sort of thing likely to suggest an imaginative course of action. And what course of action is possible if it is unimagined? (This is what the doctors will not understand.) That beautiful laughter no more than an object of envy and resentment? That wind no more than a fortuitous analogue of internal smash-up? One owes to life a more earnest commitment than that. Even this shred of life left quivering here.

Quivering from head to foot, even yet. A name is a name is a name. And at that moment, the shriek brimming in my throat, I tasted annihilation; it was like a live moth on my tongue.

Don't laugh, you idiot.

Annihilation is annihilation. Camus, this Frenchman, would agree, though his book still puzzles me and I must read further. Now, back to the stone.]

ЛЛЛ

THE BOOK in which Aspen kept his diary was a tall double-entry ledger, bound in red and stamped with gilt; in this he wrote with a sprawling, untidy hand, black billows of ink washing across the pages without regard for the bookkeeper's isograms, either the blue ones which ran horizontally or the red ones which ran vertically. He stood at an upright desk with a slanted top. He stood heavily, for he was a thickset man, and shifted his weight continually from one leg to the other. His thighs trembled in his denim jeans. From time to time his fingers brushed impatiently through his short, tangled, green-blond hair, or twitched at the shoulders of his parasitic sweatshirt. His pen scratched volubly in the room's silence.

The room was large, with a high ceiling, many-angled walls, and a slanted skylight, the panes of which had been painted sedulously black. In one corner an easel rose like a derrick, surrounded by small tables of various shapes, which were littered with brushes, tubes of paint, knives, pencils, pieces of sandpaper and steel wool, thumbtacks, magnifying glasses, paste pots, chisels, a small bust of Zachary Taylor, ash trays, coffee cups, and hundreds of other useful articles. Untidiness prevailed in the rest of the room as well. A double-size, inner-spring mattress lay askew in the middle of the floor, partly covered by a rumpled sheet and blanket; an uncloseted toilet, amid a vast rubble of books and magazines, occupied another corner; and elsewhere, resting haphazardly, a leather chair brooded with downdrawn brows, and a phonograph vegetated. Clothing hung despondently on hooks, like flayed beeves; shoes, with their protective coloring, lay doggo on the floor. A last-year's Sears Roebuck catalog snoozed unconcernedly on the radiator. Canvases were stacked, face down, in varying heights around the room, giving somewhat the appearance of broken columns; and the effect was magnified, rather than decreased, by the scrubby standing lamps which grew up here and there in splintery attitudes and by the tangled vines of electric cord which ran along the floor. A heavy stink of paint clung to everything, like bats in daylight.

Such was Aspen's room. Such, in its external aspect, was his life. The room stuck to the top of a large suburban house like a two-week-old kitten clinging to the neck of a stout woman. The rest of the house was inhabited by Aspen's family, none of whom he ever saw. A silent woman, a sort of maid, brought him his meals when he pushed a button, and attended to his other necessities. Aspen regarded her with friendly shame, but she kept her eyes cast down. He bought what things he needed to buy from Sears, except for his paints and canvases, which came from an art supply house on West 54th Street. Aspen went out only at night, well after darkness had fallen, usually at midnight or one o'clock in the morning, when he prowled greedily among the adjacent streets, stepping quickly into the shadows if a late car's head-lights threatened him, or standing inert to hear the musical gurgling of a manhole. Aspen was an artist. He had enjoyed a moderate success some years ago, but now no longer exhibited his work, which consisted of hundreds of paintings and drawings of the same stone. Not a large stone; a small stone, perhaps nine inches by five; loaf-shaped, smooth, gray with streakings of white; he had painted it large and small, crudely and carefully, abstractly and concretely, and, in short, had investigated the possibilities of the stone so thoroughly that he knew they, like his boredom, would never be exhausted. Recently, after a long period of slapdash painting, he had returned to an interest in technique. Indeed, he had begun to work his colors with inordinate care, no longer taking them straight from the tube. He preferred to blend them on stiff paper, and had found that the best paper of all for his purpose was the covers of *Partisan Review,* which he had ripped off all the back numbers he could find by burrowing through the rubble. For hours he sat on the floor under the intersecting cones of light from half a dozen lamps, squishing colors with a tongue depressor on the torn covers of the magazine. He wondered whether it might not be a good idea to grind his own pigments. At night when he went out, he would listen to the gurgling sewer and think about colors.

As for the internal aspects of his life, they were indescribable.

ЛЛЛЛ

[This is the story. Simple enough, in all truth. Fellow name of Meursault, ordinary guy in most respects, living in Algiers, working in an office (something about exports-imports, one gathers), receives, one summer morning, a telegram announcing the death of his mother, whom he had, some time (years, presumably) earlier, installed in a "home" at a place several hours away by bus. He asks for and is granted time off from the job; goes to the home; does what is required, viz. "sits up" with the body all night, in company with other mourners from the home, and then, the next day, walks in the funeral procession to the church in the neighboring village, attends the service, and stands at graveside during the interment. Point is, he remains totally unaffected. No grief whatever. His impressions during the episode, recorded in some detail, are chiefly annoyances, petty annoyances at that: the fatigue and boredom of waiting on the corpse, the unpleasant scrutiny of the other mourners, the prying questions of the warden in charge of the home, the blinding sunlight and suffocating heat on the way to the church, above all the inconvenience of everything, taking him away from his usual activities in the city. He says several times that it wasn't his fault, meaning his mother's death, the sorrow it has brought to her companions, especially the rather infantile letting-down of an old fellow, name of Perez, who had been carrying on a make-believe romance with the mother before her death; and, of course, it is perfectly true, none of it is his fault in the least.

Meursault returns to Algiers, goes swimming (his favorite activity), meets a girl on the beach, takes her to a movie (a comic picture, as it happens, which the girl had wanted especially to see), afterward brings her to his apartment, lays her, etc. She does not learn until it is over that he has just returned from his mother's funeral, but nevertheless she is attracted to him and, some time later, asks him to marry her. It's all the same to me if that's what you want, he tells her, although he makes it clear he does not love her and considers the question unimportant, not to say tedious. Tedium, in effect, seems the clue to his being. He exists only in his rejection of the customary involvements of life. Yet his attitude toward life-in-general is a curiously nonintense pleasure, which nevertheless becomes extremely intense by virtue of his simple insistence, day after day and week after week, upon it. Not very well put. The fact is, he spends a whole Sunday, for example, watching from his balcony, taking pleasure in the changing light, in his scorn of the passersby, in the ritualistic activities of the shopkeepers across the way, never stirring from his flat, unwilling even to go out and buy the necessary provisions for his supper; and elsewhere, in many passages, he records his rather highly sensitive, though never emphasized, responses to small sensual gratifications, the effects of light and color, the sounds of the city, the sea. All this, however, only up to the point where he is not engaged in the slightest necessity. His contempt for man-made "necessities," such as religion, morality, government, is supreme; but his attitude toward natural coercion, hunger, sex, the weather, etc., though less explicit, seems almost equally disdainful. Meursault is a non-participant.

Even so, he is caught up. Another tenant in his building, a scrubby type, name of Raymond, seems in need of friendship, offers pledges of lifelong devotion, along with food, wine, and intimate disclosures of his affairs. Meursault is unimpressed; but accedes, nevertheless, in order to avoid the effort of a refusal. Raymond's mistress, an Arab, has played him false, according to Raymond. There has been the usual quarrel, and Raymond has repudiated the girl, but has not, in his view, sufficiently demoralized her; he seeks a further revenge. His plan, which betrays his conventionality and jejune imagination, is to write a letter so cleverly and contritely worded that it will entice the girl to come once more to his flat, whereupon he will pretend to effect a reconciliation, embark on the customary amorous proceedings, and then, when the girl is properly stoked up, spit in her face and kick her out, a course of action which will constitute, in Raymond's view (and presumably the girl's), the ultimate insult. There is a hitch, however; Raymond cannot write the letter, he isn't clever enough. He sees at once that Meursault is the wordy type (not altogether true) and asks him to do the composition. Meursault, again acting from indifference, agrees. The letter is written and the plan succeeds admirably, except that, instead of simply insulting the girl and ejecting her, Raymond, in an access of enthusiasm, beats her, with the result that there is an uproar, the neighbors complain, and the police intervene. Nothing much happens; but the following day Raymond finds himself shadowed by several Arab men, one of whom he identifies as the brother of his now thoroughly renounced (his word is "punished") *petite amie*.

Meursault and his girl, whose name is Marie, are in his apartment at the time, and they overhear the beating and the sounds of the Arab girl in distress. But when Marie asks Meursault to call the police, he says he doesn't care for policemen.

On the following Sunday, Meursault and Marie agree to accompany Raymond on a visit to a friend who owns a beach-house. They notice that two of Raymond's Arab shadowers are trailing them. Later, on the beach, Raymond, Meursault, and Raymond's friend encounter the Arabs; there is a scuffle, one of the Arabs has a knife, Raymond is wounded. The three men return to the beach-house, and Raymond goes off to see a doctor; when he returns, he reports that his wound is not serious. He is in an ugly mood, he has a revolver. He sets off down the beach and Meursault, apparently hoping to keep him out of trouble (though this seems out of "character"), follows. When they reach the Arabs, after walking across a hundred yards of sand in blinding heat, Raymond offers to shoot one of them out of hand, but Meursault objects, in a reasonable tone, saying that it would be a poor trick to shoot without provocation. He suggests that he take the pistol and use it if necessary, while Raymond picks a fight; but the plan fails when the Arabs refuse to rise to Raymond's taunts and threats, and instead disappear to the cover of a nearby rock. Raymond is immediately more cheerful, his conventional sense of honor has been upheld, the two men walk back to the beach-house. Almost immediately, however, Meursault returns alone to the beach, in order, he says, to escape the boredom of sociability in the beach-house. He finds one of the Arabs resting half in the shade of the rock. It is the hottest part of the afternoon, the sun is blinding. Meursault continues to advance, not knowing precisely why, tormented by the fierce sun. When he comes within a few steps of the Arab, the Arab draws his knife. The sun glints blindingly on the blade. Meursault tightens his grip on Raymond's revolver; then, dazed and apparently disoriented, he fires one shot into the Arab's body. At this his mind clears; but, knowing the day has been ruined anyway, he fires four more shots, which the Arab, who is probably dead already, receives without visible effect.

End of Part One. And the precise middle, the pivot, of the novel.]

ЛЛЛЛ

ASPEN DID not omit dates from the entries in his diary because he was ignorant of them; although he lived in a tower and was an artist, the tower was by no means ivory, but rather ordinary plaster and wood, nor was Aspen himself anything but a most ordinary person: he was at pains to specify to himself that, if he was an artist, still he was a poor one. How other could he read the anguish of failure to which his painting reduced him day after day, year after year? A good artist, Aspen believed, was one whose art made him well. In any event, he was certain that to permit himself the smallest romantic pretension on the score of his vocation would be to capitulate finally and irretrievably to the dark specters of illusion.

Indeed, Aspen was alert to the world, knew the date of each day perfectly, and the news of the day as well; for he read the newspapers, the tabloids and sporting journals in addition to the *Times*, and took an interest in accounts of scandals and accidents. But "interest" is scarcely the adequate word. Aspen's need for intimations of life was a hunger, a starvation. Even the silverfish that burrowed among his rubbled books could set up a yearning in him. Dates? Simply the algebra of events; and Aspen knew many formulae, coordinates of seductions, deaths, marriages, strikes, pronouncements, wars; all beyond his room. Here nothing happened.

Time was *uneventful*. Aspen's yearning, compulsive and acute, was by necessity unquenchable, for he was unconnected with life; he was dead, and no date could fix the limit of his melancholy suspension. Hence his diary was undatable.

In his unchanging light, Aspen worked to descry the minute components of red which glowed within the gray stone and gathered toward the streaks of white, flecked by the thousand pinpoints of silica on the surface.

⊓⊔⊓⊔⊓

[The second part runs off click-click. Clockwork. Not that anything in it is, strictly speaking, predictable; yet one receives the impression (I did, anyway) that, whereas in the first part life is lived more or less in its ordinary messiness and illogicality, in the second part the chronography becomes an inevitable, illuminated progression toward disaster, going forward, step by step, with remarkable regularity and dispatch. No criticism implied; terribly true\ that at certain periods of intensity, life does assume this methodical aspect. Moreover, during the entire second half, Meursault is in the grip of the state, he is a prisoner, controlled, his slightest gesture, by the very mechanism of coercion which he had been trying, however ineffectually, to elude; and consequently, what more natural than that, in the circumstances, his life should be cast in a swifter, surer tempo. In short, Meursault is in jail, and the book ends in the immediate expectation of . . . the guillotine.

Four main episodes: the magistrate, the trial, the priest, the illumination. The first three are simple enough, they erect the architectonic opposition between Meursault, the nonparticipant, and the conventional society which enjoins his participa-

tion. Open-and-shut. The magistrate, who interrogates Meursault in the usual way after he is brought to jail, demands
that Meursault assume the conventional attitude of the criminal:
guilt. Meursault is, of course, unable to do so. He tries, half-
heartedly, to establish an amiable relationship with the magistrate, is pleased when the magistrate pats his shoulder, but
finds, nevertheless, that what the magistrate says is meaningless to him. The magistrate, on his side, attempts to elicit
some sign of Meursault's remorse, but finds none. He is
particularly upset, he avers, by the extra four shots Meursault
had released into the Arab's body, regarding them, reluctantly,
as evidence of crime committed in mere brutality. Meursault,
he intimates, is intelligent, educated, a notch above your
"average" murderer; there must be a "rational" explanation.
He ends by invoking the figure of Christ on the cross, speaking of the verity of redemption for all souls, even the most
guilt-ridden, provided a sign of contrition is ascertained.
Meursault remains unmoved. The magistrate throws up his
hands and nearly resorts to tears.

The trial: more of the same. Meursault sits, uncomprehend-
ing, in the dock. The nub of the prosecution is his criminal
nature; he is told that he is a congenital immoralist, a hopeless
case, and the evidence adduced against him is his behavior
at his mother's funeral. Indeed, Meursault begins to believe
he is under trial for that, rather than for the Arab's murder.
His friends, Raymond, Marie, and Céleste (a restaurant pro-
prietor whom Meursault has patronized and whom he regards
highly), testify in his behalf, offering their good opinions of
his "character," but their attempts are twisted against him by
the prosecuting attorney. (The procedures, incidentally, seem
odd, considered in terms of Anglo-Saxon precepts of justice;
especially the introduction of "evidence" irrelevant to the
crime with which the defendant is charged. But one assumes
Camus knows French law and is sticking to it. At any rate,
the scenes in court, like the rest of the book, are narrated in

the style of ordinary realism. Nothing Kafkaesque, or delusory, about them at all.) The trial ends with summings-up by the two attorneys. The prosecutor's is the usual rant, assertions of the prisoner's malicious intent, etc., his criminal nature, etc., etc., fitted out with a spate of self-revealing clichés. Counsel for defense, in his turn, performs no better; pleads guilty with extenuating circumstances; emphasizes the motifs of Meursault's prior unobjectionable record, his reputation as a faithful employee, his sufficient punishment in a "lifetime of remorse," etc. Meursault deems his own lawyer's efforts "feeble." The upshot, of course, is conviction.

Next, the episode of the priest, which differs, however, in an important respect. Meursault had submitted to the affronts of the magistrate and the court; that of the priest provokes an outburst, a passion, of denial and affirmation, the only passionate moment in the book, which in itself appears a re-vealing clue. (But to what? The point, first and last, is that the book is far from simple.) In any event, Meursault, who is, of course, an atheist, has refused, during his time in prison, to receive the chaplain; but toward the end the chaplain walks into his cell unannounced. A confrontation occurs, as before, with the priest arguing that Meursault, although he stands condemned by earthly justice, still has a chance of for-giveness "in the eyes" of God. Meursault, first calmly, then vehemently, denies the existence of God, rules the question of God boring and, in Meursault's circumstances, irritating, and discredits the priest's certainty of a hypothetical reality. He affirms, while gripping the priest's cassock, that the priest is scarcely a living creature and that only he, Meursault, possesses certainty; certainty of the things he has done and has not done, certainty of his crime and his punishment, certainty of his death which has been moving toward him, like a "dark wind" from the future, since the moment when he was born. In such circumstances what difference does anything make? Why search for meaning in the face of irreversible unmeaning? Nothing has the least importance; nothing, that is, except being alive, the "privilege" of living; and even this, he implies, is important only because of the immediate pleasures it bestows. It all comes to the same in the end; for everyone; Meursault, Marie, Raymond, the priest, everyone. Death. The transcendent wrong, egregiously ulterior to every category of moral understanding. There is no appeal; just as for Meursault, too, the lawyer's efforts, predictably, are futile. In his fury, Meursault grips the priest hard and shouts in his face, and the jailers come to intercede.

In these words and actions, Meursault explicitly declares what he has been suggesting, apparently without full awareness, throughout the book: the omnipresent absurdity of existence. And this leads to the brief "illumination" at the end. Topic for another day.

As for the stone, I am encouraged. Its certainty, too, is warrantable. A matter of pigments, as I suspected. Those years wasted in design, emblematicizing! But now I am in touch with the life of the stone at last. Which is one way of saying the work is more operose than ever.]

⊓⊔⊓⊔⊓

[The priest has gone, Meursault is alone in his cell again. He sleeps; deeply, dreamlessly. He awakens, and finds the stars (from his cell's window he can see nothing but a swatch of sky) and the cool night air playing upon his face. The sounds of the sleepbound summer countryside come to his ears, and there are images of the sea: night flooding him "like a tide," the smell of salt, a liner's whistle sounding. The ship is putting to sea, he recognizes, with its cargo of voyagers to a world which has passed from his concern forever. But at this point a number of ambiguous, possibly cryptic statements are introduced. I repeat them verbatim:

"Almost for the first time in many months I thought of my mother. And now, it seemed to me, I understood why at her life's end she had taken on a 'fiancé'; why she'd played at making a fresh start. There, too, in that Home where lives were flickering out, the dusk came as a mournful solace. With death so near, Mother must have felt like someone on the brink of freedom, ready to start life all over again. No one, no one in the world, had any right to weep for her. And I, too, felt ready to start life all over again. It was as if that great rush of anger had washed me clean, emptied me of hope, and, gazing up at the dark sky spangled with its signs and stars, for the first time, the first, I laid my heart open to the benign indifference of the universe. To feel it so like myself, indeed, so brotherly, made me realize that I'd been happy, and that I was happy still. For all to be accomplished, for me to feel less lonely, all that remained to hope was that on the day of my execution there should be a huge crowd of spectators and that they should greet me with howls of execration."

The Stranger. Marvelous title, beautiful idea.]

ЛЛЛЛ

IN THE waste and sorrow of Aspen's life, moments of exhilaration were not unknown. No doubt to call them "moments" is to speak metaphorically; yet they were brief, a week or two in duration, and they occurred so infrequently, no oftener, say, than once a year, that Aspen, in looking back over his debris, could regard them only as generally useless incidents, like the annual thaws of January. Nevertheless, he cherished these "moments" while they lasted. He could not say that they made life worth living; but at least for a time they lifted him out of the pit in which his being contended with itself, and transported him, like a leaf blown upward on an unexpected whiffle. He found himself elsewhere, so to speak. And "elsewhere" was, for Aspen, a delicious, forever-desired country, unexplainable and, except by luck, unattainable. The doctors, of course, recommended that these moments of exhilaration be used for ventures in the phobic world, hoping that Aspen might extend the frontiers of his confinement.

"And then?" Aspen was skeptical. "Then when it is over and I fall back once more?"

Possibly a permanent residue of gain might accrue, the doctors intimated. Aspen sniffed. "No," he said, and added that the gain would, in any case, be too small to justify the risk and suffering; besides, he should spend his "moment" of release in pursuing the objectives which he was uniquely fitted to pursue, for only in this way might a significant gain be won. And what were these objectives? To paint. To think. "But to paint *my* paintings, you see, and to think *my* thoughts. Otherwise, there would be nothing unique about it, and I should be forced to agree with you."

The last previous "moment" for Aspen had occurred, as nearly as he could remember, eighteen months earlier, and the intervening term had been an expanse of desolation, the darkest he had experienced. For some months he had believed he was dead; not in a fictive manner, but dead, a corpse. He could discover no sensation of life in his own being. Indeed, he could experience himself at all only by observing himself studiously as he stumped to and fro in his room, lifting his fluttering hands to his eyes, and even this experience was of an objective type: he was aware of himself *solely* as someone else, an object among other objects. At this time he spent unvarying days and nights against his window, seeking his life among the silent figures which moved on the visible segment of street, or among the treetops, the snow-billowed roofs, the stars. Later it seemed to him that a reversal occurred: he lived, the rest of existence was dead; he, horridly alone in a universe which had no consciousness outside his own throbbing, gigantic skull. In his agony he covered the panes of his window with black paint.

Aspen had the good sense to distinguish, isolate, and dismantle these rhapsodic systems of derangement. Good sense? He questioned himself closely on that score. To give in, to succumb, to fall: might not that be the safer, more comfortable course? Some vestigial instinct of puritanism held him back, made him frugal in the management of his small treasure of sanity. But he knew, at any rate, that, whatever the source of his anguish, it had been deepened, abominably and perhaps fatally, by errors of mind; his mind; which had been, as he was continually aware, unconditionally precommitted to interference by a "force" prior to his own. In such circumstances, his only effort could be the undoing of error. Aspen's *hope* and *despair* were his *intelligence*.

The new "moment" of exhilaration was, in fact, an interim of ten days, possibly more; the time required to read and reread *The Stranger*, and to fill its margins, end papers, and other unoccupied spaces with a looping, untidy Arabesque of speculation and wonder. Aspen's excitement roused as he read. An access of strength and well-being seized him: he who had been insomnious slept calmly and rose from his mattress with vigor; he who had been queasy ate voraciously and sent the silent woman back for seconds. He painted enthusiastically, sketched, daubed, experimented endlessly, drew hundreds of cartoons with a felt pen on pages of the *Times;* these were given such titles as "Meursault on the Bus," "Meursault and Marie Afterwards," "Meursault Upon Caliban," and so forth. With great strokes he swept the word *"Freedom!"* across his wall. Yet in his work on the stone his smallest brush moved and stopped without trembling, without support, and the web of rose-gray-silver shimmered on the canvas. He worked every day. The nimbus of his blond-green hair whirled in the lamp-light, and his heavy face swayed as if to keep the rhythm of an unheard, unknown, and unimaginable symphony.

ЛЛЛЛ

[Freedom. So long lost. I'd nearly forgotten it, in fact: the real sense of it, the sensation of it. A sinewy kind of feeling. Curious I should be reminded of it by a prisoner; this stranger, this Meursault. During the first days and weeks of his im-prisonment, Meursault suffers (and let no idiotic paterfamilias say it is not suffering) from sexual privation; and one day, when he is in conversation with the jailer, the subject comes up. "There's something unfair about it," Meursault says, "Like hitting a man when he's down." Which is, of course, precisely, exactly, the thought of the prisoner: that the interdiction of natural functions is a gratuitous addition to the penalty, an effect rationally unrelated to the cause, and hence terribly unjust. (The precision of Camus is his chief *artistic* virtue, evident not only in style and the larger aspects of organization, but also, and especially, in the way he touches the exact source of a feeling with no more than a phrase or two. One can never doubt he writes from knowledge.) But the jailer responds with a surprising truth: "That's the whole point of it," he says, "that's why you fellows are kept in prison." Meursault replies: "I don't follow." "Liberty means that," the jailer explains, "you're being deprived of your liberty." How simple, classical. And how opposed to the accepted modernism that sex and, for that matter, all nature, far from being a liberty, are an en-slavement, an inescapable determinism which creates us against our wills, first as the shapeless fruit of our parents' need, then as the misshapen *materia in qua* of our own. A churchly bias, no doubt. And the doctors, far from dispelling it, have reinforced it.

Yet, given this apparent verity, why am I subject to the unmistakable impression that, in this exchange, Meursault is the one who is free, and the jailer is the one who is deprived? Of course, the general slant of the book, evident throughout, applies here as well: the jailer, who is not only a member but a monitor of bourgeois society, is acting under the constraint of a false and grotesque morality, while Meursault has thrown off this shackle. Then Meursault is the "freer spirit"? The term is, simply and totally, laughable in connection with Meursault, who would be the last in the world to assert that stone walls do not a prison make. And he is in prison, and the jailer is not. Consequently, Meursault's greater freedom must lie, whether or not he himself would recognize it, somewhere in the region of nonobjective things.

The conversation goes on. Meursault acknowledges the truth of the jailer's point, and the jailer says: "Yes, you're different, you can use your brains. The others can't. Still, those fellows find a way out; they do it by themselves."

The next day Meursault, too, resorts to making love by himself.

Then what is the point of the jailer's observing that Meursault can use his brains? It comes to the same thing: masturbation. Not a very satisfactory "way out" for anyone experienced in sex, as Meursault is, or for anyone devoted to freedom, as Meursault also is. Yet I still know, any reader knows, that Meursault is free, and that the jailer and "the others" are not. Meursault's "brains," i.e. his power of self-reflection, of knowing what he is doing, of "objectifying himself," must be his freedom. A conventional enough idea, in its turn; but consider: precisely this power is what imprisons me, paralyzes me, and hundreds upon hundreds of thousands of others who resemble me. Can one be free simply by recognizing what, under coercion, one is doing? Can one be free even if one follows the recognition with an act of will, ordaining necessity?

At any rate, freedom. The theme, the exhilaration. And what do the simpletons know about it? Blast it, how soupily it resounds through the flannel pages of the *Times!* Freedom, freedom, freedom. Meursault knows what freedom is. Having a woman when you want one. And I know.

Meursault's intelligence and the uses to which he puts it are the factors of concern in this book, I think.]

⊓⊔⊓⊔⊓

[Turned up an inconsistency, though. In speaking, early in Part II, of his sexual privation, Meursault tells how his fantasies evoke images of women he has had, Marie and others. "The cell grew crowded with their faces, ghosts of my old passions." But considerably later, during the episode with the priest, he says that "once upon a time" he had tried to see a face, the face of Marie, "sun-gold" and "lit up with desire," against the wall of his cell, but had had no luck: he had "never" seen it. So much for precision, even that of Camus.]

⊓⊔⊓⊔⊓

[Meursault, that non-participant who appears to submit with complete passivity to the flux of experience, nevertheless keeps a certain openness, a receptivity, to the phenomena of the world; damned near to the point of tedium, as a matter of fact. He continually uses such phrases as "I noticed for the first time that," "I was struck by," "I realized," etc., etc. Of course, he is unastonished, so much so that one at first thinks he is indifferent, too; but no, he seems to be genuinely interested in what occurs around him, almost clinically interested. The "Robot Woman," for example. A stranger, a middle-aged, undistinguished-looking woman, she asks if she may sit at Meursault's table one evening at Céleste's restaurant. He agrees, noticing that she moves in a curiously jerky manner. She is excessively precise in her motions, gives her order to Céleste in a clipped, fast voice, laying out on the table the exact change for the meal, plus a small tip. During the meal she reads from a schedule of radio programs in a newspaper, and makes ticks with a blue pencil against those which attract her interest, absorbed the whole time in her own affairs. She says nothing further to Meursault. After the meal, he follows her, "having nothing better to do," but she walks too quickly for him and he loses sight of her.

Later the robot woman (as Meursault calls her) turns up among the spectators at his trial, where she studies him closely during the proceedings. But she says nothing, signals no recognition; in fact, her presence is accorded only a phrase or two.

Now, what does Meursault really think of the robot woman? And Camus, for that matter, what does he think? It isn't as simple as one might expect, for all that the woman occupies scarcely one full page in the entire novel. Nine out of ten readers, I imagine, take her to be a stereotype of bourgeois sensibility, like the others in the book, the magistrate, the judge, and so on. And no doubt the robot image supports such an interpretation, the human automaton of machine civilization; shades of Capek. I believe Camus was perfectly aware that nine out of ten readers, or more likely 9,999 out of 10,000, would make this interpretation. In a sense, he relied on it. And I also believe (twist, twist) this isn't what he meant at all.

What does Meursault say, after he has lost her in the crowd, that evening after dinner? "For a moment the 'little robot' (as

I thought of her) had much impressed me, but I soon forgot about her." True, he doesn't say he was *favorably* impressed; but he was interested, no doubt of that, he follower her, something rather unusual in his passive life; and, on the contrary, the other images of bourgeois sensibility, the judge, the attorneys, are the ones who reduce him to boredom, so completely that he nearly falls asleep during his own trial for his life. Perhaps "for a moment" Meursault has caught sight of his ideal? Notice that the robot woman does not listen to the radio indiscriminately, which is what a real robot would do, but chooses her programs with some care. Notice that she is perfectly self-sufficient, does not even return Meursault's curiosity. Notice that she eats her dinner with gusto; "voraciously," as Meursault says. And notice that her robot movements, however graceless, nevertheless are marvelously economical, sure, and swift. She outpaces Meursault: isn't that the point? Obviously, she is enjoying life immensely, *and she leaves Meursault behind . . .* !

Except that she turns up again at the trial, and is there on the last day, living, self-secure, when the sentence of Meursault's doom is pronounced.

I don't know. It's true, after all, that Meursault is interested in the grotesque, the (in his terms) opposition; he keeps a scrapbook, for instance, in which he pastes clippings of laxative advertisements and other fatuities which amuse him. Perhaps the robot woman falls somewhere in that region; perhaps not. An ambiguous case. But she is not, certainly, a simple figure of bourgeois sensibility, or insensibility. In fact, if she is taken in a "negative" sense at all, then she must embody a monstrous stereotype, the collectivity, the robot state itself, a pure lack of sensibility, which is nevertheless self-sufficient precisely *in* its grotesque capacity for unconcern; but this seems unlikely, the little woman is too slight a figure to carry such a burden. I incline more to the theory of the "ideal." But Meursault himself is uncertain.

What does Camus think? Perhaps the point is that he doesn't, that he himself is unable to say why the robot woman has "impressed" Meursault. Curious I should have been so deeply taken by Meursault. Freedom, freedom, I said to myself, when perhaps that wasn't the author's intention at all. What was it? To produce a work in which each spectator discovers, horribly, himself? But that would be mere psychotechnics, and besides, the author is far from absent. This is no "slice of life," not by any means. Quite the opposite, I'd say, a shaped, concentrated work, a stone. A most painterly novel. Camus is there. I can't help feeling, in spite of the ambiguity in Meursault's attitudes, that Camus holds a firm and steady perspective, unequivocal. To discover it seems terribly important.]

꟯ꟐꟐꟐ

[The days of good craft are ebbing. Blast it, I didn't mean *that;* though it woebegonely may come to the same thing. Some would say so. Sum who'd sigh sow. Glum wood's eye glow. Kum quat psy cho . . . What I did mean is it's ending, rounding off, the cycle of energy, and queer (blast again) how it was coupled (blast) with my feeling (blast, blast) for Meursault. Triple blast and damnation!]

꟯ꟐꟐꟐ

[Consternation overcame me. And my own foolishness. Why must the madman, in his dreadful isolation, act the clown? Perhaps for the same reason that the clown, in his dreadful publicity, must act the madman.

In any event, it *was* Meursault. To the end, to the end, I said to myself, to the guillotine, we two, carefree in the midst of the jeering mob; how that pledge sustained me! Nothing equivocal there. I got it into the stone, I think, at least part of it, though again unfinished; the feeling could not be supported longer. Flat canvas, discrete pigment. Except, I maintain, for the perfect fragment, the achievement of the incompletable; let the rest go to hell. There will be other stones.

But the blackness is general, as before.

Nevertheless, something *is* retained; at least the inclination to continue questioning; and that is an improvement.

The trouble came here: "It was as if that great rush of anger had washed me clean, emptied me of hope, and, gazing up at the dark sky spangled with its signs and stars, for the first time, the first, I laid my heart open to the benign indifference of the universe." I had been washed, too, purged by the shock of wind, swept and burnished in my hopelessness, not for the first time at all, but again, renewed in that gust of despair and terror; and I, the older, could lead Meursault onward. So I thought; it seemed as if I were doing it. But he went away from me, lost me. Benign? Oh, Meursault. "To feel it so like myself, indeed, so brotherly, made me realize that I'd been happy, and that I was happy still." Of course, happy in that moment; but brotherly? What brotherliness in that universe? And is that the image of a man?

Back to the pivot. Meursault is walking down the beach. It is a fierce day, truly fierce. "The sand was as hot as fire, and I could have sworn it was glowing red. . . . And each time I felt a hot blast strike my forehead, I gritted my teeth, I clenched my fists in my trouser pockets and keyed up every nerve to fend off the sun and the dark befuddlement it was pouring into me." Was that benign, Meursault?

Then there is the black rock near which the Arab is lying, a black rock with a "cold, clear stream" behind it and a "tinkle of running water."

The Arab draws his knife, the sunlight glints from the blade with a blinding flash, the sweat from Meursault's forehead deluges his eyes, everything reels in the fiery heat and the sky cracks "in two." Meursault pulls the trigger of his pistol. Why? *Why did you shoot the Arab?*

Later, to the magistrate and the court, Meursault remarks that he had no intention whatever of shooting the Arab, the Arab was nothing to him. He seems clear in his mind about the actual event: he did shoot the Arab and he is to be put to death himself as a consequence of his crime; but the fact is Meursault doesn't appear to know why he shot the Arab. Is he completely volitionless? Is the crime simply another aspect of absurdity bearing down upon him from without? Is it merely the result of his having permitted himself, the nonparticipant, to be caught up in the foolish, determinative cycle of contingency? But this would be a denial of his very existence, his self, his consciousness, which is precisely what he seems to be most earnest about affirming. No, the end of the book does not shed as much understanding upon the middle as one is inclined to think.

Back, again, to the pivot. There are two possible explanations. First, that Meursault has been so exhausted by the heat that he simply must reach the rock and the stream of water in order to save his life; the Arab, with his knife, stands in the way; Meursault shoots him as a means of saving himself. But all this talk about glaring sun and fiery heat is, after all, *somewhat* exaggerated, *somewhat* rhetorical. Meursault is a young man, in the vigor of his best years, and he has not, in plain fact, been straggling for days over the sands of southern Algeria; he has been strolling for as long as ten minutes, possibly, on a Mediterranean beach. The hyperbole is intentional, the rhetoric itself has meaning; and what they mean, most of all, is that something is happening on this beach which does not meet the eye. The second possibility, then, is that Meursault is simply crazed momentarily, that the demon is on him; it's a case of absurdity all right, but not the petty absurdity of involvement in Raymond's affairs; rather, the absurdity of an inhuman compulsion, the sun itself entering Meursault's skull, driving him, usurping him. Meursault, could it happen to you?

Never! A-ha, I thought so, no mystical claptrap between us two, eh? Besides, when you fired the first shot everything cleared, didn't it? The sweat fell from your eyes, the light slackened? Yet you tripped four more shots into the body of that Arab, "and each successive shot was another loud, fateful rap on the door of [your] undoing": so you have said. A bit theatrical, not really quite like you, but what does it mean?

No answer.]

ЛЛЛЛ

[Necessity of reading everything Camus has written.]

ЛЛЛЛ

[Necessity of reading everything written about Camus.]

ЛЛЛЛ

NATURALLY, ASPEN, being the person he was, did not press to the last letter of attainment the program of reading which he had recommended to himself; but he was neither demure nor dilatory in essence, and he took to his studies with a good will and a certain half-anxious vivacity. Seated on the toilet, with open texts scattered around him and two lamps craning above him on either side, he concentrated on the word. Squares of limp tissue, inserted among the pages of the books, marked passages to which he wished to return, although he quickly lost track of the cross-references he had established. Nor was his note-taking more successful: the leaves from his yellow legal pads, smeared with the gaudy secretions of his ball-point pen, drifted and settled among the ruins of former enthusiasms. It was a difficult but not arduous venture; Aspen felt that he made headway. In each book by Camus, Aspen was struck by the same quality that had seized him in the narrative of Meursault, a sense of concentrated urgency that belied the simplicities of the narrative itself and drove the reader to an effort of penetration. At one point Aspen wrote in large script on a yellow pad: "Personality of Camus: poised on the brink of terror: hoverment: never permitted to reveal itself in the medium: known, or unknown, in imagery solely: images of doubt which nevertheless convey no hint of irresolution."

Impelled by his discoveries, Aspen went to his stone, touched it, turned it, soothed it for the thousandth time with his fingertips, and went to work. But he did not abandon his books.

Much that Aspen read regaled him; it was a feast of cogency. But the commentaries he found chiefly useless and naïve, thrusting them angrily aside. Even parts of Camus seemed perversely contrary; some of the images which inverted or contorted a conventional meaning appeared to do so merely for the sake of scandal. "Adolescent!" and "*Maniéré!*" were terms that appeared from time to time in Aspen's marginal notations. When he came to the end of *The Myth of Sisyphus*, he copied out the last sentence: "One must imagine Sisyphus happy." And he added: "What an appalling ignorance of stones!"

But the seriousness, the success, and the purpose of Camus

drove Aspen on. A voice was arising from the wreckage of the world, addressed to the living. "No," it was saying, "no more. We have had our fill. No more fictive absolutes, no more dandyism and cruelty. Away with them!" and Aspen, who had nothing, who was bereft of everything but his stone, responded with eagerness. For he was an American; not one, certainly, whom the patriots would have recognized as an exemplar, but still an American; and the spark of Yankee practicality smoldered in his consciousness, to which he offered alternate thanks and curses. Could he submit his single remnant, his stone, to the absolutes that override individuality: God and history? "No," he murmured, adding ruefully: "Neither the one, nor the other." But man existing in face of absurdity, man daring to call himself the "absurd man," this was something else again, a new hope; and if Aspen had not yet learned enough of Camus to avoid the word "hope," he instinctively took it to mean a possible existence, a relative survival, an assertion howled in the face of defeat, which Camus also would have approved.

One of the mottos pinned to Aspen's wall was: "*Prima facie* the world is a pluralism; as we find it, its unity seems to be that of any collection." Such a world, the world defined by William James, offered, Aspen thought, a place for imperfectibility and radical failure, a place for suffering; such a unity left room for the disunited.

Yet Aspen could not rid himself of romance; desire for ultimates seized him with a quivering paralysis. Those oldsters, the Europeans who were his fathers, artists who had converted style to reality, poets who had leapt from the abyss of nihilism to the crest of self-created, self-discovered meaning, lovers of moon and blood, they who had sired his art in the spasm of their perfection, could he deny them, could he deny the yearning that throbbed in the marrow of his love? If he thrust away the sanctity they had conferred upon him, what else could clothe him? And he, the paralyzed captive, could he ever hope to act if no action were ordained? Had not William James also written: "The ultimate test for us of what a truth means is the conduct it dictates or inspires?" Could this new European, this outsider at the heart of chaos, this Camus, offer a resolution?

At any rate, Aspen was not the only one who was puzzled by Meursault. Camus as well suffered from the inscrutability of the man, and sought him through a succession of studious and reproachful inquiries: *The Myth of Sisyphus, Caligula, The Plague, The Rebel, The Fall.* Aspen, seated on his toilet, leaned to the texts with the attentiveness of recognition. In these words he found what he had often said to himself: "Carry on, *mon enfant*, the idiocy cannot be all yours?" What else had kept him alive these seven years? Yet the new words were, after all, new; sounded with a pang of strangeness in his ears; faded into silence at the very moment when instinct was piercing at last into the heart of meaning. Something was wrong; many things were wrong. For one, this Camus was too damned healthy, he with his love of the sun and sea. Yet the man had tuberculosis! More contradictions, more obscurities, there was so much to be asked. If only, somehow, he could get to him, could come up to him like a friend, affably and intelligently, no fencing, no delicate evasions, and say, "Look here, Camus . . ."

⊓⊔⊓⊔⊓

[Is it possible? My gods and demons!]

⊓⊔⊓⊔⊓

IN THE spring of the year, with his stone and his kit, with a phial of Librium capsules in his left-hand coat pocket and a phial of Nembutal in his right, on a jet transport privately chartered at immense cost, quivering unseen in the Atlantic night, Aspen was brought to Camus. The note which he left for his family was as follows: "Carry on, *mes enfants*, the idiocy cannot be all yours."

part two

ASPEN WAS frightened. The room was small, white, and prickly, furnished a flaking veneer. The presence of Camus, who was sitting on Aspen's cot, seemed too near, too large. (The room and the presence, in truth, recalled to him another room and another presence from a time when his being had been wrested away from him.) The two had been talking for some time. Aspen's eyes roamed the cracks in the plaster or studied the tarnished ormolu of the unused stove. His hands made fluttering movements. Camus, on the contrary, was suave, calm, brown, and remarkably handsome; stylish, as well. Aspen had known that the other was a person of the theater, even at one time an actor, but he had been unprepared for anyone who resembled, to such a degree, the stereotype of a star.

Camus smiled, very faintly. "You are still ill at ease?"

"Yes."

"Obviously. However, I had not thought I was such an ogre."

"No, no."

"But . . ."

Aspen sighed, nervously. "Well, you see, you *are*, in a sense; but . . . so is everyone."

"I see," Camus said; but added that he did not altogether understand, in spite of the explanations Aspen had attempted earlier. "The state of mind you describe is foreign to me."

"Yes, one gathers as much from reading your books."

"Why do you say that?"

"Well, you have plenty of . . . *odd* characters in your books, some totally whacky, off their beans, but no one I recall who suffers from the type of anxiety I have known all my life."

"Fear is fear. Of course, clinically speaking . . ."

"No. Let's leave the clinical interpretation out of it; I agree it isn't useful in this context. Though for that matter there is one general concept that seems to apply."

"Yes?"

"Repression. So many of your people seem afflicted with repressed anxiety, which then pops out in peculiar, unrecognized ways, like the old fellow in *The Plague* who spends all his waking hours counting dried peas and passing them from one pot to another."

"The asthma patient."

"Yes. He must be driven by something, something hidden, something completely irrational. Mustn't he?"

"He has his reasons."

"They all do."

Camus smiled again. "I mean he has his reasons in the novel."

"You had your reasons for putting him there? His actions have an objective meaning which you objectively assigned to them?"

"If you like, though I imagine it isn't quite as arbitrary as that."

"Well, then, what about Meursault? He must..."

"A stronger person. Much more difficult in all respects, I think. I really wouldn't care to speak for him."

"No, I suppose not. Who would? Still, he did exist. And he did do what he did."

"Shot the Arab?"

"Yes, and left an account of it, such as it is. I mean it's a marvelous account, of course; but, on one hand, unclear, and, on the other, since it exists, debatable."

"I suppose so." Camus got up from the cot, paced a few steps, and stood with his back against the recessed, blue-shuttered window, propping one elbow on the cracked marble sill. "You see, my relationship with Meursault ... well, extremely close at one time, no doubt, but now? I'm not so sure."

"Tell me. Even then, when you were so close to him, did you completely understand him?"

"I thought I did, though not in a way I could ever define analytically. But why Meursault? After all, his was a case that happened . . . once upon a time, wasn't it? At any rate, there are others."

"I've offended you."

"Not at all. But I would like to know."

"Oh, it's hard to say, hard to explain. I don't mean the others, some of them, aren't more important; in fact, I'm sure they are. Yet Meursault is the one who compels the attention, *my* attention. Not only because he left himself partly unexplained, but because of . . ."

"Of what he did? The gratuitous crime?"

"But was it gratuitous? Lots of people have said so, I know. And the gratuitous crime was in the air, so to speak, almost a fad, a post-Nietzschean style. A fellow like Genet, your exact contemporary, could make up an entire mystique on the basis of it; and before that, in America, there was a book called *King Coffin*. . . . Yet there was something about Meursault which won't permit me to believe his crime was gratuitous, not in the proper sense of the term. And there is something about you that confirms my feeling. You were the author."

"Yes, I was the author. I'll tell you frankly, I had nearly forgotten Meursault; not the fact of Meursault, of course, no one would let me forget that, but the presence, the man himself. So many people had talked about him, so much foolishness. I had a sense of failure, do you understand?"

"Too well. I . . ."

"Of course. But I don't see that repression has much to do with Meursault."

"You don't mind going back, then?" Aspen grimaced.

"No."

"Well, I think that's just the point: repression has nothing to do with Meursalt. He left an account of his sensations at the moment of the crime; the heat, the light, the giddiness. Possibly we should interpret this as a form of repressed anxiety, yet Meursault gives no clue to fear. Certainly he is not afraid of the Arab, and he doesn't appear to be afraid of anything else. Yet later . . ."

"Precisely. Later, in prison, he says that he has been aware of his own death every moment. And we are agreed that death, one's own death, is the only thing to fear."

"Yes. Death must be the origin of all fear. Immortals know no anxiety; that is the established principle. And if Meursault has always been aware of his own death, flowing toward him like a wind out of the future . . . isn't that the expression he uses? . . . then if he has always known this wind, it must have been blowing at the moment of the crime as well."

Camus shifted, and stood straight against the wall. "Yet he never shows evidence of anxiety as you know it?"

"No. He is neither repressed nor anxious. In my experience one must be . . ."

"Your experience. But we are where we started. Remember, I said I found your experience foreign to me. I suppose the question is, why?"

"The clinicians . . ." Aspen stopped. "We can't escape them, it seems. But I think they would say it is a question of feeling the presence of death. The immediate, terrifying presence. For Meursault, for you, death may be certain, but it still lies in the future; it is at a remove. Hence you are able to forestall the brunt of your anxiety. For me, however irrationally, the death blow is always about to descend."

"Something like that, no doubt."

"But if Meursault acts neither from repressed motives nor as a consequence of overt anxiety, then what is it? He does shoot the Arab, once and then four times again. Was it gratuitous? Would Meursault bother to attempt an explanation of something which had no explanation? And at such length too? There they are, one shot and then four, the cause of his undoing?"

"Undoing?"

"Yes. That is his word."

"Have you read my text?"
"The French, you mean? No."
"Better have a look at it."

⊓⊔⊓⊔⊓

[Of course, of course. *Et c'était comme quatre coups brefs que je frappais sur la porte du malheur. Malheur.* How could it mean "undoing" when Meursault has been aware all along that he was "undone" from the moment of his birth? A ridiculous word besides; Meursault would never use it. A simple (!) case of mistranslation in the distinguishing word of the whole book, the word at the very center of the book. The diacritical word, so to speak. What a muddle!

The French-English dictionary gives a number of meanings: unhappiness, misfortune, bad luck, etc. All centered on unhappiness, which is the primary meaning, as everyone knows; and without doubt this is what Camus intended. No fiddle-faddle or equivocation whatever; no poetry. And it makes all the difference in the world. It means, quite simply, that the second half of the book is a story of Meursault's unhappiness, not of his doom, and that his crime is a "cause" of unhappiness, not of doom. This helps a good deal in assaying the nature of the crime, obviously.

Undoing, indeed! His doom was long since sealed; the meaning of the crime, the nongratuitousness of it, must be sought elsewhere. Isn't this the whole point? Existence, Meursault's and everyone's, is a condition of chronic metaphysical diathesis; which is only a whopping circumlocution for absurdity.

But look at the whole sentence in English. "And each successive shot was another loud, fateful rap on the door of my undoing." Aside from the point that he utterly spoils the in-

cisive simplicity and purity of the French, where does the translator find his "successive," his "loud" and "fateful," even his
"my"? And what was the necessity? "Door of unhappiness"
would have had precisely the literal, unemphatic meaning
which Camus intended. "Door of my undoing" is sheer melo-
drama. Aspen, never trust a translator.

At any rate, Camus is fine. I mean the man as well. Quality
of gentleness, humaneness, a sort of detachment. And humor,
more than I had expected. Never sufficiently remarked before
the extent to which the impersonal view is prerequisite to the
compassionate view . . . He said he'd come back again, possibly
tonight. Seemed upset, in a way, by my trembling and what it
meant, and didn't realize (although I told him) that he is the
first person to whom I have spoken more than ten consecutive
words in . . . Lord knows how long. I did it, I managed.
Poorly, but intelligibly. And the credit, if he only knew, is
his. Magnificent to be talking, no doubt of that, a kind of liber-
ation, a burgeoning, and there's almost a quality of felt radiance
in the timbre of my voice; but not simply in *my* voice; my
voice together with the rest, this strange room, his changing
expressions, the hearing, thinking, being. Oh, it's impossible to
explain! The room is alive. I suppose the danger now is that I'll
talk too much, I can feel myself letting go; but, I must say, it
is a joyful danger.

He seemed genuinely interested in the stone, too.]

⊓⊓⊓⊓

"NO, I agree with you, the translator has missed the point,
which is rather discouraging when you consider that of all
people he must have read my text with particular attentiveness." Camus was in good form; he sat on the cot with his

back against the wall, his arms folded, and his head cocked to one side. "A question of relative failures: his and mine. No? On the other hand, perhaps his error isn't as crucial as you make it out to be."

"Why not?"

"Meursault maintains his attitudes with a fair degree of consistency throughout the book, doesn't he? The mistranslation of one word, even what you call a pivotal word, ought not to destroy the whole effect."

"Well, it can throw you off. It certainly threw me off."

"Yes, I suppose so. And I am not at all pleased, frankly. If I have any technical merit as a writer, it is that I choose my words with care, extreme care; I mean each one to say precisely what it does say. No one has a right to change them. Where is your book?" Aspen passed his copy of *The Stranger*, open at the last page of the first part, to Camus, who read a few sentences and then read one aloud. " 'I knew I'd shattered the balance of the day, the spacious calm of this beach on which I had been happy.' At least he doesn't change Meursault's reference to happiness there, and that ought to have been one indication to you. But 'spacious calm'? That doesn't sound like Meursault; too ordinary. It doesn't sound like me either. What is the French?"

Aspen read: "*J'ai compris que j'avais détruit l'equilibre du jour, le silence exceptionnel d'une plage ou j'avais été heureux.*"

"Of course. 'Destroyed,' not 'shattered.' And 'exceptional silence.' The precise terms. Well, what can you do? Nevertheless, the point is . . ."

"I suppose the point is," Aspen said, picking up the sentence that Camus let drop, "that Meursault speaks in terms of happiness and unhappiness throughout the book. Not explicitly; I think he does that only at the end of the first part and again at the end of the book, the two climaxes. But his intention is reasonably clear elsewhere. In the second half of the book, for example, when he complains about prison life, the loneliness, the monotony, the sexual privation, and so on, this is entirely a question of his unhappiness, his immediate, so to speak existential, unhappiness. At any rate, he does not suffer from what people usually call a moral feeling; he has no remorse, no compunction. And at the end of the book when, as a consequence of his outburst against the priest, he finally achieves a degree of clarity and resolution within himself, he speaks of having found happiness again, of having refound it. You remember, of course; the point where he recognizes in the starry sky a quality of the universe which he calls 'benign indifference.' I have read the words many times in English, and once I copied them out in my notebook." Aspen thumbed the pages of the French text, and read aloud: "*Comme si cette grande colère m'avait purgé du mal, vidé d'espoir, devant cette nuit chargé de signes et d'étoiles, je m'ouvrais pour le première fois à la tendre indifférence du monde. De l'éprouver si pareil à moi, si fraternel enfin, j'ai senti que j'avais été heureux, et que je l'étais encore.*"

"Exactly. He had been happy, and he still was."

"Not for long, however."

"No, presumably even Meursault, or especially Meursault, would be unhappy with his neck under the knife. But he had chosen the manner of his death. He knew how it was going to happen and, within narrow limits, when. This is more than most of us can manage. In other words, Meursault could confront the event of his death with great concentration, and could maintain his humanity and his defiance, if you like, to the very end; quite consciously, too."

"Meursault chose the manner of his death. Do you mean it literally? Was that why he shot the Arab?"

"Who can say? Perhaps some such motive was at work, unknown to Meursault. We are told that we all subscribe 'unconsciously' to these inclinations, these 'death wishes,' although I myself have never placed much stock in the theory."

"No, that is clear." Aspen, who was sitting in a gray wicker chair before a card table covered with books and papers, leaned forward. "I say, do you mind if I sketch you?"

Camus smiled. "You know, secretly nothing pleases me more than having my picture made, though I've never told anyone. I wonder, is it simply vanity? Do you think so? Is everyone like that?"

"The lucky ones are. Some of us fight our likenesses like poison. But really, I don't think vanity has much to do with it. More a question of the security of the self, isn't it? Sometimes it takes a brave man to look in a mirror."

"Maybe so. Anyway, go ahead if you like. What do you have in mind?"

"Nothing. Artists are always looking for a picture." Aspen picked up a pad from the card table, and took the cap from a felt pen. "Besides, it helps to loosen me up if I have something to do with my hands."

"I see."

"Going back to Meursault, we have agreed, in any event, to exclude hidden motives, at least in the Freudian sense, and with good reason. But even though there does seem to be a sense in which Meursault is not aware of himself completely, he nevertheless is straightforward in his relationships with himself. In *all* his relationships, for that matter. Am I correct?"

"Evidently."

"Then he cannot commit a crime either in order to hasten his own death, or to force his own unhappiness; both intentions would be equally repugnant to him, and the one because of the other. This connects up perfectly with *The Myth of Sisyphus*. Incidentally, do you consider *The Myth* and *The Stranger* more or less coeval, so to speak, the essayistic and fictional sides of the same coin?"

"They spring from the same sources, yes."

"In *The Myth* you say that man, confronted with the certainty of his own death, acknowledging this certainty continually and at the same time acknowledging that the certainty invalidates all purposive concepts of experience and renders life absurd, in these circumstances you say that man can pursue only what you call a 'quantitative' ethic; in other words, he can only pack as much experience as possible into his life, trying, on one hand, to enjoy each experience fully, and hoping, on the other, that his life will not be cut short by some factor of untoward contingency."

"I doubt I spoke of hope. On the contrary, I think I clung pretty narrowly to the notion that man's condition is hopeless, radically and unalterably hopeless, isn't that so? And I insisted that hope is a category of fiction, a non-sense, a conceptualization derived from non-knowledge. And I insisted, further, that part of the 'absurd' ethic is a lucid recognition of hopelessness, and acceptance of it. Long life is desirable, surely; but it's a matter of luck."

"Yes, yes, that's it. Okay. But it is difficult to see how you can avoid hope if you give yourself the alternatives of a long life or a short life, and then say that the outcome is solely up to chance."

"That isn't hope. That is desire, or longing."

Aspen inclined his head. "As you say, you choose your words with care."

"I try to, of course. But ultimately that is incidental. What I choose with care are ideas, and my method of choosing, as with most writers, is by naming; or by renaming, defining. You might say that the whole point of *The Myth of Sisyphus* is the distinction between legitimate, inevitable desire and illegitimate hope; a man who is truly aware of absurdity will never permit one to turn into the other. On the other hand, this conversion is natural in everyone, it occurs whenever our vigilance against it flags for so much as an instant; it shows up, for example, in the common idiom which you just fell into, using 'I hope' to mean 'I wish,' which is all the more reason why the absurd man must guard against it."

"That is your paradox, isn't it?"

"What do you mean?"

"Well, it seems to me your idea of happiness is very intimately bound up with nature; a happy man is a man acting naturally. You speak in terms of sex, eating, swimming, the country, the sun, and so forth. Am I right? But then the danger, the absurdity, arises from this same natural condition, either in men or outside them. Like the natural danger of converting desire into hope. That's the whole history of religion, isn't it? And it kept men happy for five thousand years or more, and drove them to despair and frenzy and murder, too. Maybe it is the history of art, of your own writing? The natural act works both ways, in other words, creating happiness and everything that is desirable, but at the same time leading to death and all other aspects of absurdity, including human error."

"You are very perceptive."

"Hardly. But one can't help noticing, especially when it hits so close to home."

"You mean your own troubles?"

"Yes, indeed. Very much so. And Meursault's, too; you have no idea how close that man is to me."

"To all of us."

"Is that true? I suppose it must be, so many people have taken the trouble to argue about him."

"I'll tell you something I've noticed; you could demonstrate it if you took the time. Every discussion of Meursault ends by considering him as Christ."

"Rather shocking, in a way."

"That Christ should turn into Meursault?"

"No, that Meursault should turn into Christ, such a far thing from what he wanted."

"Jesus of Nazareth probably didn't want it either. No sane man would. Tell me, do you consider yourself sane?"

"Unfortunately, yes."

Camus dropped his eyes, smiling in ironic complicity. "Let

me see your sketch," he said. "Yes, a strong line, even bold. Do you realize that the work never resembles the artist?" He held the sketch pad at arm's length. "In this case, I'm not certain it resembles the model either. Do I really look so much like a stone?"

Aspen's huge face squirmed with embarrassed laughter.

⌐⌐⌐⌐

"WE HAVE been skirting round and round the point, circling it, almost stalking it. Strange how I have receded into the presence of Meursault. I almost feel younger, and I almost don't like it; a damaging confession. In spite of one's alertness, one comes to rely upon one's certainties, which then turn out to be only habits. Meursault is a doubtful person in many respects; is and was; and so was I. Which is one reason why I feel, quite unaffectedly, that the author's reflections are of less value than the reader's. What do you really think?"

"About the shooting of the Arab? An extraordinary complex of thoughts and feelings, all told; a concatenation; it would take hours merely to make a beginning. Do you know why Meursault seized my imagination so convincingly at first? Because I had an experience which seemed very close to Meursault's experience on the beach. Oh, I agree, what could be more preposterous: two people, as dissimilar as Meursault and I, sharing any experience whatever? Yet that, you see, is precisely what struck me as particularly important. And I don't mean I shot anybody, either; I agree with Meursault, the shooting was incidental."

"Go on, tell me about it."

"Early spring. Night. A dark wind, damp and surprisingly powerful. A suburban street, a grove of dark pines up here."

Aspen blocked out these images with his quivering hands. "There am I, you see, an absurd figure, bent against the wind and rain, fearful, scurrying along. Across the street and beneath the light, a man and woman, dressed for a party. The woman laughs, and at that exact instant the wind strikes, suddenly, viciously, a blow infinitely more violent than the rest. The pines bellow. I feel a scream bursting in my own throat like a . . . like a panic-striken frog leaping for his pond, like a bubble of asphyxiating nothingness rising from the absolute zero at the pit of the universe. No metaphor is ever right. At any event, I turned and ran. You see how it was?"

"Yes."

"Superficially, the analogy is clear enough, no doubt. For me the wind and rain played the role which, for Meursault, was played by the sun and heat. The difference was that his was a daylight episode while mine was after dark. A considerable difference, come to think of it; perhaps the whole difference, i.e. Meursault was well and I was ill, the light and the dark. But we have agreed to disregard these factors. The analogy can be pushed a step further, I think. Meursault, it seems, had some reason, although the precise degree is uncertain, to fear and resent the Arab, who stood, holding his knife, between Meursault and the cool shadow of the rock and the tinkling brook beyond. In the same way I had some reason to fear and resent the couple who were on their way to a party; they represented to me a certain freedom, gaiety, warmth, self-possession, and so on, call it happiness, which I had not had for many years, if ever, and which I desperately wanted. That was an extreme moment for me, in which the compelling factors of my existence were brought together with concentration and symbolic clarity; my need and my incapacity, my desire and restraint. If I had had a gun in my hand, I might very well have shot that man and woman, in the same mood of obscure frenzy that saturated Meursault at the moment when he shot the Arab. Luckily for me, I did not have a gun."

"Luckily for them."

"Of course, but that's something else again. The point is that the analogy between Meursault and myself can be advanced still another step, at least I believe it can. For Meursault, resentment of the Arab was clearly an insufficient motive for his act; we have agreed on that, and in any event Meursault himself says, later on, that the Arab meant nothing to him; even if he was then referring primarily to the Arab's contingent relationship to Raymond's contingent relationship to Meursault, I think he also meant to include the actual meaning of the Arab *per se*, so to speak, during the confrontation on the beach. After all, Meursault was *temporarily* blinded and dazed by the sun. He was a strong young man and he had been on the beach, as we have said, for only a short time; he could not have been literally sunstruck or parched. And beyond that, resentment would always have been an inadequate motive. Have you not pointed out somewhere that resentment is a concomitant of envy, that it is not an assertion of what one is but a shrewish appeal for what one lacks, that it is a weak, passive emotion, not suited to the motives of intelligent men?"

"Toward the beginning of *The Rebel*, I think."

"Then obviously resentment is not the motivating factor in Meursault's crime, and he is quite justified in emphasizing the effect on him of the heat and light, even to a point which seems, at first, highly exaggerated. It *is* exaggerated in terms of the physical effect; but in terms of something else, perhaps the metaphysical effect, it is not exaggerated at all. And in my own case, I like to believe that the same reasoning applies. Resentment was *not* a factor in my plight; the man and woman meant nothing to me, whatever the doctors say. It is demonstrable, for instance, that now the sound of wind, not the sight or sound of a woman dressed for a party, excites in me the recrudescent hysteria of that scene, and even though I know the doctors would explain this as a subconscious associative link between the woman and the wind, I insist that the wind is primary. The woman's laughter was, for me, only the sunlight glinting on the knife-blade. Should I, should Meursault, should anyone, be consigned to the damnation of clinical predictability? It is too much. Aren't we human beings, aren't we, that is to say, beings susceptible to all the amplifications and discriminations of experience that have accumulated during ten thousand years of civilized sensibility? After all, we may not approve what we call civilization, I determinedly don't, but still it is a remarkable development, not to say rarefication, and we, the human beings, the men and women who compose it, are not only its creators and its agents, but its products. As for me, I find it exceedingly degrading, at this stage of the game, to be treated as if I were operating with the sensibility of the Stone Age. Degrading and, what's more, unjust."

"As a matter of fact, you don't need to convince me. I . . ."

Aspen fluttered his hand. "Sorry. That speech had been rehearsed a good many hundreds of times, I'm afraid."

"And never delivered?"

"Not till now."

"Then it wasn't wasted. But go on."

"Yes, let's dispense with side issues. Do we agree that the bright sun for Meursault and the dark wind for me were the causative factors, symbolically speaking?"

"Provisionally. But do you notice how you have fallen into Meursault's usage to describe your own experience? He spoke of the 'dark wind' that flowed to him from his future."

"That's so. An acute expression. Except that for Meursault, it had been, up till the end, something rather remote; he also calls it a 'breeze,' I think, and speaks of it as 'slow' and 'persistent.' "

"Yes."

"Well, for me it was something very near, a hurricane. The point is that at our respective moments of crisis Meursault and I were exceptionally open to experience in its malevolent essence, to the universe in its aspect of destroyer, to the absurdity of consciousness confronted with reality. I take it this was not simply a question of our own deaths, though that might have been enough, but rather of all deaths, death as the functional principle of being; Meursault, in his flare-up with the priest, speaks not only of his own death, which was to be, after all, somewhat out of the ordinary, but of the leveling force of all death upon everyone and hence upon all values. And since both Meursault and I were atheists as a matter of course, we could not pin our fear and anger on God, as did the metaphysical rebels whom you discussed in *The Rebel:* De Sade, Lautréamont, and the rest. For us death appears simply as a force of reality, mechanistic, determinative, as implacable and mindless as the multiplication tables. Hence for us the tyranny of the absurd was disclosed in the blazing sun and the blasting wind, attributes of mindless reality. The reason why these moments of crisis occurred, and why they occurred when they did, the clinical reason, in other words, does not need to be explained; probably it is, at root, unexplainable. As you have said, knowledge has only a limited utilitarian value, and most of what people usually call knowledge is fictive anyway, or rests on hypothetical foundations. All we know, all we need to know, is that moments of crisis, moments of compacted moral, metaphysical, and psychological force, do actually occur; and that, as a matter of fact, they are not in the least uncommon. They must have been the substance of a great deal of what was called mystical experience."

"Better not to generalize about that," Camus said, speaking in a mock-judicious tone.

"Voice of experience? Oh, well . . ." Aspen blinked, ostrich-like. "We are among friends. The really interesting point, to my mind, comes now. Here are two men at their moments of crisis, crushed by a radical, exigent manifestation of absurdity, something over and beyond the 'normal' relationship of moment-to-moment awareness and fortitude which ought to exist between man and absurdity. Something, in other words, which neither man can manage; both are dazed momentarily by the total force of reality concentrated upon them. In such circumstances, only an instinctive response is possible. There can be no question of taking thought. And what, then, does Meursault do? He pulls the trigger of his revolver and shoots the Arab. By this I understand a gesture of instinctive revolt. Meursault, with the last scrap of his afflicted being, his oppressed intelligence, is striking back. If his intelligence had been totally destroyed, incidentally, he would have aimed his revolver at the sun and fired away in rhapsodic dementia. He would not have been the first to do so, by any means. But in his dazed consciousness he retained just enough of his faculties to recognize that shooting the sun would be futile. At the same time he knew that he must make some gesture of revolt in order to regain his own existence as a self-contained consciousness, and he also knew that this gesture somehow must assert, on some rudimentary level of meaning, the fullness and seriousness of his intent. He shot the Arab. He was, of course, too far gone to enter upon any of the usual considerations apropos his civilized, or at least civil, relationship to the Arab; all that was impossible. But he made his act of revolt, and he made it, within the elemental terms of the situation in which he found himself, real and unmistakable. His crime was neither gratuitous nor premeditated; it was merely necessary. Do you agree?"

Camus nodded, without commitment.

"Of course, this is where the analogy between Meursault and me comes to an end." Aspen fluttered his hand. "Under the coercive omnipotence of absurdity, Meursault revolted; I only fled. With, it should be added, a scream of terror rising in my throat. And this is why, it must be why, I found Meursault, immediately, instinctively, such an attractive figure. You know, I was absolutely bowled over by the force of the man?"

"Force?"

"Yes, I know it sounds odd. I myself have spoken of him in terms of his passivity, what I called his 'non-participating' temperament. And yet I always was aware of his force. It must have been in that shot, that revolt, which I never could manage. Yes, it would be ridiculous to say I could have shot that woman, even if the revolver had miraculously appeared in my hand. I'd much more likely have shot myself. And I cannot help believing, in this curious involuted way, that Meursault makes by far the more attractive appearance. What do you think?"

"To tell the truth, I never cared for the fellow."

"I thought not. I begin to care less for him myself. In fact, my liking for him began to decline some time ago, and just now, while I have been speaking in praise of him, it has declined, unaccountably, even further. Yet I cannot avoid the presumption that Meursault succeeded where I, miserably and repeatedly, failed."

"Still, Meursault is dead and you are alive."

"Yes." Aspen sank back in his wicker chair. "Yes. We have a way to go, don't we?"

⊓⊔⊓⊔⊓

ANOTHER EVENING the discussion flagged. Aspen was hunched over his sketch pad, his hair tousled and damp. The night air detained the heat of the day, and summer was well begun. Camus sat as usual on the cot, his feet, crossed at the ankles, on Aspen's dusky counterpane. He had removed his jacket, opened his collar, pulled his tie askew; his shirt cuffs were loosened and turned back over his forearms. In silence he played intently with a silver cigarette lighter, flipping the top open and shut.

Aspen looked up from his work. "What is it? Are you disturbed by something?"

"Moderately. As much as seems possible these days. I've been wondering. About our ages, among other things. You are younger than I."

Aspen, leaning back in his chair, mumbled assent.

Camus cupped the cigarette lighter in his two palms, and shook it. "But not much?"

"Ten years more or less, I imagine. Why?"

"Yet you think of me as a member of the older generation."

"Yes, I suppose in a way I do. Not on account of age, though. At least other factors have a lot more to do with it. What you've done, for instance, your accomplishment, all these books." Aspen's hand wavered toward the card table. "While I have done practically nothing. And then there's the question of nationality, or rather cultural location. You know, to Americans even the children of Europe seem somehow old and wise. You've been in the thick of it, while we've been . . ."

"On the fringes?"

"Not exactly that, not any longer. But I think Americans do still feel that somehow they can escape when they want to. The old colonizing syndrome: when things get too thick, pull up stakes and move on. Not much more than a feeling now, of course, although you'd be surprised at the number of American intellectuals who periodically cancel their magazine subscriptions and move to the mountains."

"Refusal to commit themselves to reality?"

"Not exactly that either. In fact, most Americans would be outraged by the suggestion. But no doubt they do feel subconsciously that when things come to the very end, to the choice between lying about one's convictions and standing up to be shot, then they have an out somewhere."

"While we poor Europeans are stuck?"

Aspen sniffled. "You sound almost pleased."

"I am, in a way. I have always understood that my ideas

sprang from a consideration of man, which is to say myself, at the extreme of the human condition, what you call 'the very end.' Not that the ideas themselves are extreme, quite the contrary, but they arose in extremity; and this is what I have always known. Now you confirm it, but from a somewhat different, unexpected point of view."

"I see. But what were you thinking when you asked about my age?"

"It isn't flattering."

Aspen picked up his sketch pad. "I don't mind."

"Then tell me this. Are you never quite simply horrified by Meursault's crime?"

"Of course, that." Aspen put down his pad. "I think I . . . well, the fact is, no. Not horrified. I recognize the horror of it, I know that perhaps I ought to be horrified, I see in principle that the shooting of the Arab is contrary to what I believe to be right on every ground of training, temperament, sentiment, and sober reflection; yet I do not feel the horror. Never did, not even on first reading. But that's an esthetic factor, isn't it? A condition imposed by the novel?"

"I should think . . ."

"I mean it's an established principle that every work of art is self-limiting; you can't choose one objective without precluding others. Would it be possible to write a novel in which Meursault, narrating his own story, reveals himself exactly as he is, in a context of the agreed-upon correctness of his opposition to conventional views, and at the same time to cast the whole work into a larger mold of a priori ethical concern? This would mean too many layers of opposition. You can't have your cake and eat it too."

"Yet your description fits my intention precisely."

"Oh."

"You see why I think of us as two generations? I had been counting on that ethical concern, I had been counting on a sense of shock. But you don't have it. You pass over the shooting of the Arab as if it were the commonest thing in the world, as if you could step out your door any morning you like and find a shot Arab along with your newspaper. Yet we Europeans are actually the ones who have had most to do with corpses, Arab and other. You in America, I'm told, have banished them almost magically. How do you account for the fact that we have kept the ethical concern which you somehow have lost?"

"We have been shocked in books too often."

"Ah, the blunt answer. And you have put your finger on it, too, I imagine. For contrary to the usual supposition, the truth is that Americans have taken much more seriously to books than Europeans. In the unreality of your wonderland you have turned to the fictive objectivity of art and literature as to a documentation of fact: Dadaism, Surrealism, the thrillers, everything. And in consequence you have dulled yourselves to actual shock, to death and absurdity. Isn't this what you mean, really, by the American's vestigial intuition of a way out?"

"Maybe, maybe."

"Don't take offense. We are working to recover you, to retrieve you. And we shall. Do you conceive that anything but recovery is in order for someone who believes that he has failed where Meursault has succeeded? You can go no further in *that* direction, at any rate. Tell me honestly, taking the book as a whole, I mean its whole image, the impression it leaves on the mind after the episodes have receded, can you consider Meursault a success in anything beyond his own last-minute self-realization, which comes far too late?"

"Well, if you put it that way . . ."

"Aspen, Aspen, don't be so damned earnest. You've been thinking about Meursault so hard that you have practically lost sight of him. Of the supreme, obvious fact about him, anyway. Don't you see? Meursault is stupid."

ЛЛЛЛ

"OH, I was piqued a bit, no doubt; but not seriously. Besides, it's unimportant. What struck me, shocked me, was your saying Meursault is stupid. Can you mean it? To be honest with you, I always, first and last, felt quite the opposite to be the case. At one point I even put the whole question of the novel in terms of Meursault's *intelligence*, and the use he made of it."

"I was laying it on rather thick."

"But what made you do that?"

"Annoyance."

". . ."

Camus got up and emptied an untidy ash tray into the stove with the brass ornaments. "At your being so damned sold on the guy."

"I see." Aspen hunched behind his sketch pad.

Camus returned to the cot, adjusted the ash tray meticulously among the ravines of a crumpled newspaper, and lighted a cigarette. "What are you sketching?"

"As a matter of fact, the stone."

"Don't be difficult, Aspen. Life is far too short already."

Aspen brightened. "That's true, isn't it?" He looked over the top of his sketch pad. "But I still say Meursault is intelligent; moderately, anyway. And Raymond and the jailer, among others, agree with me, remember?"

"Quite so; almost everyone finds him a cut above average. I don't argue with that, not in the least. As I say, I was laying it on. At the same time, however, it is possible to use the term 'stupid' in a way that doesn't contradict the ordinary notion of intelligence. You agree that intelligent people often behave stupidly?"

"Of course."

"That's what I meant, or something like it." Camus exhaled a jet of smoke toward the ceiling. "In a sense, you know, Meursault's intelligence is a point against him, not a point in his favor. An intelligent man ought not to place himself in such a predicament. In short, an intelligent man ought not to be unhappy. Which means that your formulation of the problem is quite just, after all: the question is not so much Meursault's intelligence as the use to which he puts it. Or fails to put it." After a moment, he added: "Is that better?"

"I'm thinking," Aspen replied, peering at his sketch pad. "One of the things I'm thinking is that last night I talked too much. Why don't you take the floor for a while?"

"Fair enough. A couple of points do occur to me, as a matter of fact. First, I agree, in a general way, with your analysis of Meursault's crime, as far as you carried it. I don't say, mind you, that I had your precise terms, your diagram, in my thoughts when I was writing, and living, that episode; I mean your rather one-to-one equivalence of the hot sunlight and the absurd. We are dealing with a work of art, after all; and although I was functioning in the same general scheme of attitude and feeling as that which you have described, I think the imagery I used is irreducible to exact references. I hope so, anyway. But, speaking broadly, the notion of Meursault's crime as a gesture of revolt against the absurd, to use your language, would be acceptable, I imagine, to any perceptive reader. The question then is whether or not the gesture was successful. You have raised the question yourself, but you answered it wrongly, or at least it seems to me you did; and it also seems to me that your judgment in this case has been impeded by too close a reciprocation with your own predicament."

Aspen said nothing, and Camus, after a pause, went on: "There is a concept which occurs repeatedly in *The Myth of Sisyphus*, so often, in fact, that the critics have complained about it: I mean the concept of lucidity. Suppose that there is a certain type of 'natural man' who is unconscious of himself and of his death, who lives from hour to hour and day to day; and suppose that, as long as he is provided with the necessaries of life, he is happy. As a matter of plain truth, this is more than a supposition with me, it is a conviction: I have known such people. But once the factor of intelligence is admitted, then the train of anxieties appears in its wake: awareness of self, awareness of death, awareness of radical doubt, awareness, ultimately, of the absurdity of existence. At once the intelligence begins searching for what you Americans call a 'way out,' a means of evading itself and making an intuitive leap into an ultraintelligent posture from which it can resolve its anxieties through an act of faith. For me, and I presume for you, this would be inadmissible; it would be an arrogation to our intelligence of faculties which it does not possess. Instead, we must work with our intelligence as we find it, and we must concentrate resolutely upon the things of which we are actually aware, the factors of absurdity. Only by retaining in consciousness a steadfast awareness of absurdity can we perceive the 'values' in life which the 'natural man' takes for granted; and this retention is what I call lucidity.

"What remains to be decided is the extent to which Meursault is lucid, and I very much doubt that a precise answer is possible. Of course, he is far more lucid than most; he resolutely and repeatedly denies the 'way out' offered by conventional attitudes. We see this on the occasion of his mother's death, when he refuses the trite condolences tendered by the staff of the old peoples' home, and we see it at every step of the way thereafter, up until Meursault's violent rejection of the priest's more serious but nevertheless equally conventional solace. Moreover, Meursault goes out of his way, sometimes, to sharpen his awareness of the conventional evasions which society practices in the face of absurdity, and to quicken and strengthen his repudiation of them. He spends a good deal of time simply observing the follies around him, and, for that matter, the exemplary actions, too. Do you remember the nurse on the way to his mother's funeral?"

"Yes."

"A sensible woman. And Meursault himself is sensible enough to recognize it. He remembers what she says to him, precisely that there is no 'way out,' and repeats it to himself later on, in prison. Still, it's chiefly the follies that attract Meursault's attention, which shows that he pretty much resembles the rest of us. He even keeps a scrapbook, in which he pastes particularly charming specimens of hypocrisy. More important, we know from his own casual remark about his past that at one time he, too, had been an ambitious young man, a student and then an office worker, a conventional type, seeking success in conventional terms; but at some point, we are not told when or why, he dropped his bourgeois sentiments and changed his attitude toward existence. Presumably, at that time he made a considerable advance in lucidity. The question is, how far did he go?

"Not far enough, at any rate. Is there any evidence, until we come to the final pages of the book, that Meursault is consciously aware of the ultimate source and meaning of absurdity, what we may call the metaphysical issues? None. On the contrary, he appears to be largely unaware, to be suspended in a state of half-lucidity between the condition of the 'natural man' and the condition of the fully absurd man. His opposition, his nonconformity, his self-exclusiveness, his nonparticipating disposition (as you have called it), his revolt, in short, is predicated solely on his sensibility; on matters of taste, so to speak, and of social taste, at that. There is a good deal in the book, I think, which suggests this, but the main evidence is the crime itself. Because if it is, as we agree, a gesture of revolt, then it is indubitably self-negating; an abortive revolt which destroys itself. It must be. In the first place, it is self-negating because it plunges Meursault into unhappiness and eventually cuts short his life, while we have said that happiness is just what the absurd man is looking for, and a long life, too, if he is lucky enough to get it. But the second and far more cogent observation is that Meursault's gesture of revolt is self-negating immediately and in itself; for if it is a revolt against absurdity, against death, how can it simultaneously inflict death on another person? Meursault's crime, which is incidentally a quite real crime, is self-contravening. A gesture of revolt against death and against the absurdity of an existence subject to death unavoidably establishes the value of the life of the person who makes it; but the value must at once be transposed to the life of every other person as well, since everyone is faced with the same absurdity. Hence a gesture of revolt against death which at the same time imposes death is an act committed in a state of radically imperfect lucidity."

"Radical imperfection is the human lot, isn't it? Constituent to absurdity itself?"

"In that sense, yes. Imperfectibility is radical in life, that is, rooted in it. But I was using the term in a looser, but justifiable, application. We are practical men, after all, and a sufficient lucidity is certainly not out of the question. It was not out of the question for Meursault, whose predicament at the moment of his crime was far from inscrutable. A sufficient lucidity would have suggested to him, as the best affirmation of his revolt, precisely the act which you disallowed on the score of futility: he should have fired his five bullets at the sun."

"It would still have been futile."

"Lucidity excludes hope."

"I see." Aspen had put down his sketch pad; he was re-

clined deep in his chair, fingering the braided wickerwork
of its arm. "I see. At any rate, I begin to see. But Meursault
nevertheless came to a sufficient lucidity in the end."

"When he was virtually under the knife, yes. And I dare
say one must not deprecate any access of lucidity whatever,
in the face of ubiquitous absurdity. But Meursault's lucidity
was brief, the happiness which it permitted him was con-
stricted. You and I, practical men, can scarcely find Meursault's resolution satisfactory."

"I suppose not."

"But do you see why I have been dismayed, appalled, by
the way in which you appear to pass over the crime of Meursault, the fact itself? Just as Meursault passed over it? He
was right, of course, to acclaim his own sense of innocence,
which was, in effect, that of all mankind; we are born in a
state of noncomplicity with the arrangements of absurdity.
But he was wrong to disclaim, or disregard, his guilt. Do you
remember, he realizes it only in the courtroom, long after
the crime, when the hatred of the crowd makes him see that
he is, in their minds, 'guilty.' But it is a shallow, technical
guilt. The plain, undispellable fact is that Meursault killed
the Arab. In doing so he put himself *on the side of death*, he
put himself in the same camp with the priest, the judge, the
magistrate, he joined his enemies. Ultimately, of course, he
destroyed himself. I'm not saying that his final lucidity, in
prison and virtually under the knife, is of a piece with the
conventional scene of self-recognition which sentimentalists
believe to be essential to the drama of the condemned criminal; on the contrary, Meursault remains, within his own
limits, pure; yet there is something a trifle too . . . what
shall I say? formal, ingratiating, theatrical, punctilious . . . ?
Well, you see what I mean. The point is that Meursault killed
the Arab, but apparently the point was not made. The novel
fails."

"Perhaps the reader fails. Or the age."

"Finally, of course, Meursault betrays his failure in his own behavior after his crime. A genuine revolt gives the person a certain self-integrity, a clarity and distinction of inner bearing. I am inclined to call it dignity, even though the word has been so much distorted. In opposition, lucid opposition, one becomes crystallized, so to speak, one is delimited and identified. But nothing like this happens to Meursault. Quite the contrary, he is scarcely a person at all. He submits without demur to the wildest misinterpretations of the police magistrate and the court. Indeed, he is quite ambivalent in his feelings toward these people, he even appears, at several points, to wish to make friends with them. Only when he becomes angry with the priest, after his trial and after his condemnation, does he achieve dignity, and then, as I've said so many times, it is too late. That moment, that outburst against the priest, is Meursault's genuine revolt, the consummation of what began without lucidity in the shooting of the Arab. And mark this difference: the Arab is dead, but the priest goes away living.

"As you have pointed out, Meursault is passive throughout the book, I believe you called him a non-participant, and even in the shooting of the Arab he can hardly be called a participant in any proper sense. Only at the very end does he rise to his single active, self-asserting moment. Perhaps I can allow myself a generalization? A man living in lucid awareness of absurdity can never be passive in essence."

Camus fell silent. Finally Aspen said: "All rather shocking. And beautiful. And puzzling. As you are interpreting the novel now, it seems like a masterpiece of satire against conventional manners and ideas, in which the satirist is the narrator, who himself is apparently in error during most of the book. What holds it all together?"

"I throw it back to you: what holds anything together?"

"Possibly its limits?"

"Possibly."

⊓⊓⊓⊓

"MAY I read you something I found this morning?"

"Of course."

Aspen picked up a large book, and opened it to a place which had been marked beforehand with a flattened cigarette. He read aloud: " '[In acting] with dignity the oppressed contains himself, affectedly, within the bounds that have been set for him and that he cannot overstep even if he wanted to. He remains in his place conspicuously when nobody has requested him to leave it. Dignity makes passivity a challenge and presents inertia as active rebellion. It is liquidated whenever conditions exist for an actual struggle.' " Aspen replaced the cigarette between the pages, and tossed the book clumsily on the card table. "A somewhat different slant, eh?"

Camus nodded. "Who wrote it?"

"Sartre."

"I might have known."

"Why?"

"Sartre . . ." Camus closed his eyes and pressed his fingers briefly against his eyelids. "I'll tell you about Sartre. My friend, my foe. He is the most brilliant man alive; without question; and a firebrand to boot. Who can help liking him, loving him? Quite simply, he is moved by suffering, deeply and honestly. A rare quality now; even the children are losing it, have you noticed? But, of course, you are an American. What shall I say? Sartre, in his zeal, in his compassion, in his fire, commits himself to procedures which I conceive to be in error, the error of the age, perhaps the error of all ages. It has been commented on often enough, in all truth. I mean he permits the ends to subjugate the means, the desired eradication of suffering to entail additional suffering. Well . . ."

"Yes. Go on."

"Perhaps this, too, is unavoidable, part of that radical imperfectibility we were talking about. I'm not sure anyone . . . The point is, here is a man with a brilliant mind and an extraordinary gift for writing who permits both these faculties to be turned to propaganda; and by 'propaganda' I mean the distortion, the manipulation, the subjugation, however unintentional and unperceived, of fact. Not mendacity, mind you; the term means nothing in connection with such a man. But simply the condescension of man to reality, when in fact the relationship should be, and ultimately is, the other way around. This fragment, for instance. May I see the book?"

Aspen handed it to him.

"Yes. It seems to me Sartre is using a commonplace idea, a received idea, if you will, which he knows perfectly well, if he stops to think, is unacceptable. Customarily people say that the different affections, such as dignity, despair, joy of living, etc., are different parts of the soul, different humors. But the truth is that they are the whole soul taken at different moments and in different attitudes; and since they are the whole soul, they each contain the others, each affection is pregnant with the seed of all other affections, and indeed they do 'give birth' to one another. This is why one man may describe a particular affection in positive terms, while his opponent, by the slightest alteration of terms, may transform it into a negative description. Such is the case between Sartre and me with respect to dignity. And I must say I am attracted to his viewpoint far more, I suspect, than he is attracted to mine. After all, who approves of dignity? It's a shabby thing, isn't it? Everyone knows that. With what do we associate it? With petty officialdom. With walruses and tombstones and certain types of mushrooms. What could be more despicable? Yet the dignity which I was recommending bears a slightly different cast from that which Sartre mocks. It is less an appearance than an accomplishment, less a posture than a conviction. It is self-possession, self-integrity, self-containment; and it is these things considered in the light of their opposites, the loss of self, the dispersion of consciousness, the invalidation of particularity. You see how easy it is to destroy language? 'Dignity' has not one referent, nor even two, but dozens."

"Isn't part of the difficulty the fact that Sartre is talking about social and political revolt, while you are talking about what you call metaphysical revolt?"

"Of course. Though that is only a temporary way out, since both of us insist that our theories of revolt are consistent in all applications. But let's take Sartre's comment sentence by sentence, and apply it to our terms. 'With dignity,' he writes, 'the oppressed contains himself, affectedly, within the bounds that have been set for him and that he cannot overstep even if he wanted to.' True enough, except for the implications. In metaphysical terms the 'bounds' of the human condition are established by death, by absurdity, which no one can overstep; and hence we are certainly oppressed. But the dignity I had in mind, although it may produce, as one of its issues, an affection, that is to say, an emotional stance, certainly is not itself an affection; it is not generated 'affectedly.' On the contrary, it is the work of lucidity, as I have said so many times. 'He remains in his place conspicuously when nobody has requested him to leave it.' I should prefer to say, 'He remains in his place lucidly when someone very important has asked him to leave it, namely, he himself.' Do you see? And the next sentence goes to the heart of what we have been saying about Meursault. 'Dignity makes passivity a challenge and presents inertia as active rebellion.' But we have seen, with great clarity, I believe, that Meursault had no dignity as long as he remained passive and inert, and that he achieved dignity only when he at last was goaded into a genuinely active revolt, when he attained lucidity. As for the last sentence, 'It is liquidated whenever conditions exist for an actual struggle,' that is a complete confusion of terms, to my mind. To oppose dignity to struggle is to eliminate the meaning of both. Naturally, within the metaphysical context, the conditions for struggle, in Sartre's sense, *never* exist; but Sartre's sense is distorted. What he really means is not struggle but hope. In the metaphysical situation, the conditions for struggle, without hope, obtain preeminently and permanently; and this lucid, hopeless struggle is precisely the source of dignity. But . . ."

"But?"

"One can't help sympathizing with Sartre's distrust. 'Dignity' is a threadbare term, and we need a better one."

Aspen thought for a moment. "It seems to me you have been taking advantage of hindsight, not only now but especially in your comments on Meursault. Haven't you been applying to *The Stranger* concepts which weren't developed until you wrote *The Rebel?*"

"Perfectly true. But is that so bad? Must I think about Louis XVI solely in terms of the philosophies of rationalism and the psychologies of associationism which were prominent in his time?"

"No, I suppose not."

"Another point you might raise in objection, if you wished to. I have been saying things about Meursault, as I realize very well, which contradict other things I have said at other times and places. But that is the marvelous thing about a living fiction, isn't it, a fiction that separates from its creator and takes on its own internal dynamism? Like a myth, it embodies all interpretations, and sustains them in a kind of limpid equipoise."

"In which case *The Stranger* is becoming more and more alive."

⎍⎍⎍⎍

"I'VE BEEN thinking."

"Thinking what?" Camus, who was reading a newspaper, turned a page, shaking the paper smartly to make it fold in the middle.

"Hmmm. Not thinking. Brooding, more likely." Aspen was squiggling with a pencil on his sketch pad, making totem poles. "Hard to get youself set up for thinking, isn't it?"

Camus smiled. "What are you brooding about then?"

"Meursault, naturally. And myself, I suppose; my thoughts always revert to myself. Do you blame me?"

"What do you mean?"

"A lot of people might put it down to self-pity. Or worse."

"A lot of people . . ." Camus shrugged.

"The truth is, you know, I think my own case, in some senses, is more useful than Meursault's, more generally applicable. Do you see what I mean? My case is exaggerated, no doubt, but still more or less characteristic, the garden variety. While Meursault is . . . well, exceptional, wouldn't you say, pretty far removed from the ordinary run? Have you ever really known anyone like Meursault?"

"Yes."

"Oh? But perhaps I shouldn't be surprised. Who was it?"

"Nobody you know."

"Meaning none of my business? I'm sorry."

"I wouldn't have put is quite so brusquely."

"The truth, just the same. Will you overlook it? I don't mean to be the prying sycophant."

"Nothing of the kind."

"Anyway, I do feel the need to recapitulate; for both of us,

Meursault and myself. Do you mind?" Without waiting, Aspen took up the discourse, speaking in stronger, measured tones.

"Here we have two men, both aware, each in his own way, of the radical absurdity of existence; and to each comes a moment of crisis when absurdity, appearing in symbolic forms, bears down with exaggerated intensity. One, Meursault, commits an act of revolt, but since he lacks a sufficient measure of lucidity, his act fails, with the consequences we know. The other, so far as outward appearances go, commits no act of revolt whatever, but he is nevertheless more successful than Meursault; at least this is the inference which seems to be justified by your remarks, and I must say I am considerably bucked up by it, even though I was acting, probably, with no greater lucidity than Meursault. However, a further paradox arises immediately, since the second of the two, this miserable Aspen, cannot claim to have found any particular happiness as a result of his success, whereas the first, Meursault, the one who has failed, makes just this claim at the end of his autobiography. A partial resolution of the paradox, of course, lies in the fact that Meursault has not *altogether* failed, just as I have certainly not *altogether* succeeded; in the course of his narrative Meursault breaks through to an ultimate lucidity and turns his ineffectual gesture of revolt into a genuine act of revolt. But something more than this is required for a full explanation. We need more exact definitions of the concepts of revolt and happiness . . ."

"Yes?"

"You are with me so far?"

Camus nodded.

"Okay. On the question of revolt, we can safely leave aside, I think, the political corollary, since we both, being leftists, agree pretty well on the practical course to be taken, and especially since we both agree that the political aspect of your thought is a necessary inference from the metaphysical considerations, just as Sartre's ethical and psychological hypotheses are necessary outgrowths of his commitment to revolutionary politi—"

"That is going too far. Both Sartre and I, I'm sure, would have to say that you are oversimplifying dreadfully."

"Let it pass. The question is, what is revolt? The answer: it consists of two phases. First, a vigilant awareness of death and of the absurdity which the fact of death creates in the relationship between the individual consciousness and reality; this is what you call lucidity. Second, an equally vigilant rejection of complicity or acquiescence in the scheme of a reality regulated by death; this, in effect, means a rejection of all absolutistic modes of thought and conduct, all philosophies of the whole, since these inevitably override the claim of the individual part and hence ally themselves with death. The existentialists say that existence is prior to essence, and you have insisted that the absurd man is a relativist. On the other hand, you have been careful to point out the distinction between your position and that of traditional humanism, which organizes reality anthropocentrically; you insist that a lucid awareness of absurdity will always acknowledge the wholly contingent, adventitious role of consciousness in the universe. Nevertheless, you and the humanists would find yourselves side by side in the larger intellectual conspectus, since you both generally insist that the starting point for all procedures of validation is the individual consciousness."

"You sound more like a philosopher than Sartre."

"You flatter me. Anyway, we are able to characterize revolt as neither an act nor a program, in the narrow sense, but a vigilance, a tension, a continual flexing; in short, a resolute nonacquiescence in reality, practiced in lucid awareness of reality. At the same time, of course, absurd revolt does issue in well-defined acts whenever the opportunity arises, and it is never passive, never inert. It will even take form, in the course of many lives, as a more or less programmatic, though never doctrinaire, mode of behavior. How is that so far?"

"Acceptable. Rudimentary, but acceptable."

"I must stick to rudiments, otherwise I'll get lost. As it is, I am about to lose myself anyway, I expect, because the problem of happiness seems much more difficult than that of revolt. We can begin by saying that happiness is a product of lucid revolt, which means that part of happiness is dignity; and I don't think we need say any more about that than we have already said. But happiness also, you have said, is pleasure, joy, the life of the senses, a bodily exploitation of nature, sun, sea, sex, and so on; it is submitting oneself to nature, that is to say, to reality. But reality is absurdity; reality is the universe regulated by death. How can you submit yourself to that against which you are in lucid revolt?"

"You are taking a too restricted view. There is death, of course, but also life. You are commiting a monism. You are—"

"A-ha, that helps. Because, you see, I remember just enough from my schooldays to add that a dualism is simply another form of a monism. Isn't that true? It is somebody else eliciting the contrary absolute to the absolute you have just offered; it is 'polarity,' as they say nowadays; it is absolutism compounded, the Hegelian vise. As determined relativists, we must throw it out; throw out life-death, happiness-unhappiness, the benign and malevolent universe. William James said that the unity of the universe is only that of any collection, an epigram I have liked very much. What do you think?"

"Mainly I think the danger of absolutism is not quite as acute as you make it out to be. Why can't we conceive of dualities which are not absolute dualities? Absolute in the philosophical sense, that is. You have a right hand and a left hand, and they are absolutely right and left, if you want to use that term; but this doesn't mean that everything else in the world has to be right or left, too. As a matter of fact, people just naturally do think in polarities, without giving undue significance to them. People live in a state of tension between two fears, two desires, two obligations; it is always two.

And this tension is extremely important, not only to the individual but to the species. Of course, it can turn into ambivalence and paralysis; but the safeguard against this is lucidity. The lucid person may perfectly well submit to and reject reality simultaneously. Remember, submission, as we are using the term, does not mean surrender; in fact, it really isn't submission at all, it is taking, possessing, getting what is pleasurable while you can. And the lucid person, fully aware of absurdity, will find that his awareness not only permits him to enjoy whatever pleasures he can find in reality but actually makes those pleasures more important and consequently more intense." Camus raised his hand. "No, let me make another point before we go on. Our discussion has somehow slipped into outworn categories. Remember what absurdity is. It is total meaninglessness; nothing has any value, not even happiness, in absurdity. The happiness we are talking about has nothing to do with the bliss of other people. It is simply whatever happiness is possible in a meaningless world. A few days ago I was saying that from our point of view Meursault's happiness at the end of his life was not very satisfactory; but remember that Meursault was quite right in calling it satisfactory for himself, because it was all that was possible in his circumstances. And that is the most that any of us can look for."

"Yes, I see. But do you believe in death-in-life?"

"A romantic term; but yes, essentially I agree to it. What else was Meursault describing when he told about his first weeks in prison?"

"And in Meursault's case, his growing lucidity was enough to dispel it." Aspen frowned, concentrating on his form of expression. "But can you not imagine a perfectly lucid person whose lucidity itself instilled such fear in him that each act of pleasure, each submission to reality, experienced in the shadow of death and meaninglessness, is changed from an act of pleasure into a spasm of foreboding and pain?"

"I should say that such a person is not lucid. Fear is part of absurdity: fear, shame, humiliation, ignorance, failure, in short, the human condition. The lucid person is aware of his own fear as a part of absurdity, and takes his happiness in spite of it, because of it."

"Ah, well, I see no way to beat your lucidity, it rises above everything. But tell me, do you think it is possible for a person to be lucid at the point of sexual orgasm?"

Camus smiled. "No. And I'm astonished you haven't pointed out the similarity between orgasm and the circumstances of Meursault's crime."

"What? It never occurred to me. For heaven's sake, what is sexual ecstasy, if it isn't happiness?"

"A kind of oblivion, isn't it?"

"And sleep? Dreams? Fantasies?"

"The same."

Aspen sighed. "You leave too many things out of account. Oh, not out of your account, but out of mine. I remember the passages in which you have insisted that your way of looking at things is only a possible way, a personal way. And yet I can't help feeling disappointed; disappointed and at the the same time worried, goaded in some dark manner. It seems to me that there is a fundamental contradiction between your concepts of revolt and happiness, yet I can't quite grasp it or define it. Until I do that, I'll never be able to . . . to do whatever it is I have to do."

"Will tomorrow be too late?" Camus spoke wryly, but gently. He stood up and went to the door. "In any event, don't paralyze yourself. Perhaps the principal object is not a resting point, but just the sort of struggle you are engaged in. In itself it is a rebellion; and the results of rebellion will show themselves to you, never fear." He opened the door. "Until next time then?"

part three

THE NEXT time, as it turned out, was delayed six weeks or more. High summer came upon them; the warmth of the season, not uncomfortable, entered and influenced Aspen's room: the stained plaster softened, the blue shutters put on a tone of ivory. Camus was called away. "Unexpectedly," he said on the phone; something had come up. "See you in the fall?" Aspen replied that of course he would be looking forward to the next meeting, and he wished him *bonne recherche*. Camus seemed amused. Aspen reproached himself for his nervous *gaucherie*.

At first, Aspen was disappointed, disconsolate, even, at times, frightened. He had come to rely upon his friendship with Camus as a source of help if it were needed; someone who could charter the plane and whisk him to the airport, dispelling the unflankable, impossible barriers, if the necessity to escape should arise. The fact that it hadn't arisen did not diminish for an instant Aspen's inner, unspoken dependence. Now that the dependence was broken, Aspen fell prey, as in the past, to moments of panic, moments when his immense danger smote him with frozen hysteria. The heavy silver spoon laden with its scollop of canteloupe would halt, for example, three-fourths of the way to his lips, and poise there in cataleptic rigidity while his mind pitched and staggered under the passing terror.

The days, however, preserved their steady cadence. No crisis occurred; and soon Aspen found that his moments of terror were no longer chronic but merely vestigial, as if his mind, newly emboldened, were calling up remembered demons that had lost their ferocity, like a nurse who, for the sake of fond complicity, recalls old bedtime spectres to a child who has outgrown them. The miracle had happened: Aspen was feeling better than he had for years. True, the manic delight, the phase of excess, had ended long since. But now he discovered a deeper, surer strength. It was still too soon, far too soon, to rejoice; yet Aspen believed, without knowing entirely why, that his new strength would endure, although naturally many ups and downs were still in store.

He ventured, for the first time, outside his room, which was in the suburban home of a jobber in hardware, who had, poor fellow, fallen on hard times. It was a question of his parents' illnesses. Aspen visited the kitchen; a word, no more, an attempted smile, a request: a bit of string, some soap, anything that came into his head; and then, headlong flight again. But soon he found himself sitting at the deal table, taking coffee with milk, a glass of wine, five minutes of gossip, ten minutes of household trivia, half an hour of the weather. From this, of course, the garden stretched no more than a rifle shot away, and the fields beyond, the stream with its clumps of osier, were found to lie on this side of the moon. Aspen discovered himself, with easel and paintbox, perched by the stream or on the brink of the hollow. "A bloody landscape painter," he remarked to himself. "All I need are the tweeds."

Aspen was charmed by the sunlight most of all, the light of high summer, which blazoned the willows and shimmered on the hay.

As a matter of fact, he called in the local tailor and had himself measured for two suits. Not tweed, however; one was raw silk, the other unbleached linen. And he took to combing his hair, to shaving every day, even on Sundays, and to saying "good morning" and "good evening." The sun darkened his face and lightened his hair, and he saw in the mirror that he had become an average, ordinary, homely sort of guy. He was enormously pleased, and sent the wife of the jobber to town to buy him a handful of ties. Her assortment was a hairsbreadth less than hideous; Aspen, examining them, chuckled with delight.

All this was quietly joyful, modestly exciting, and Aspen savored his luck. Nevertheless, his room remained his refuge. The sketches of Camus had been fixed to the walls with transparent tape, a couple of dozen faces looking down, strong and black; they had all been done with the felt pen. The best of them combined a fluidity, elegance, and strength which were right for the subject, and even those that had not turned out so well were interesting for the differences of attitude and expression they portrayed. As the summer declined, as the light slowly altered from opalescent to amethystine, Aspen bent over his card table, thrusting back the litter to make room for his big account book; and the gallery of his friend's countenances gazed down upon him in varying demeanors of approbation and concern.

ЛЛЛЛ

[All right then, blast it, here it is:

DEATH.

A dirty shame!]

ЛЛЛЛ

[Yes, shameful; no mistaking it. Yet something cracked inhabits this shame, something false. A double shame. Why did I need such bravado to inscribe the word? Why was my sense of embarrassment so disturbing that I could write no

more and had to close the book? Why do I resort to facetia-
tion? A question, once more, of clowns and madmen? No
more than that? Or less? Why was I ashamed, *I*? Did I have
anything to do with it? Did we, did anyone? Why is there
such evasiveness everywhere? Why bashfulness, why furtive-
ness? Are we ashamed of our fear, for God's sake? Isn't it
more likely we are ashamed to find ourselves in such a dirty
place, a world where a thing like this can be permitted?

A scandal.

As when the emperor who distrusted his philosophers
ordered them to convene in the public square and then came
and emptied the contents of his chamber pot in their midst,
saying, "There, gentlemen, have a look at that."

We lower our eyes.]

ﬂﬂﬂﬂ

[Death,

     death,

          death,

               death,

                    death,

                        death,

                             death,

                                  death.]

ﬂﬂﬂﬂ

[Perhaps a point in favor of our age, the age that has shaped
us, beginning with Pascal or Blake or, really, whenever you
like, is a disposition among certain people, few but increasing

in number, to confront this sense of their own *shame* with courage and forthrightness, to discuss it, to investigate its meaning, and to refuse the evasions (or to try to) which have been associated with it in the past. Perhaps. At any rate, Camus seems to me the perfect representative of the type. Whether or not he is also a paragon, a leader, I don't know; and really, I don't care. He is the only person I know or know about whom I call genuinely, completely, and seriously modern. This is all the more important when one considers that his point of view is allied, as he says explicitly and proudly, with what we suppose to have been the founding temperament of Western thought, the spirit of Athenian intellectualism. All of which doesn't mean that he hasn't made mistakes, taken on more than he could handle, permitted rhetoric and obfuscation to eclipse certain crucial points, and so on and so on. The commentators have expounded his flaws, and will no doubt continue to do so.

The commentators, however, have said nothing, as far as I know, about his failing which bothers me the most, because it is, I suppose, not truly a flaw at all in terms of the formal disciplines of argument. It is simply this: Camus, among so many others, begins with death; it is the foundation of his knowledge of reality; from it arise all his convictions about the world and the self; and yet his work contains no discussion of death itself. It is taken for granted. True, he has composed many scenes of death, some deeply shocking, such as the death of the little boy in *The Plague* or the description, in the essay on the guillotine, of what happens after the blade has dropped. These passages produce in me what they were intended to produce: retching, followed by dismay. In esthetic terms, they work beautifully. But in looking back upon them, I find I have not been enlightened by them and in looking back upon my life, I find I have never been enlightened by anyone on the subject of death. The physiology of it, for example. I know next to nothing about it, which strikes me now with a certain astonishment. My ideas are primitive, and I expect

largely nugatory. Does anyone know? I suppose only a
Lazarus with a medical degree could give us the absolute
straight dope. Yet something must be known. Why is it
suppressed?]

ЛЛЛЛ

ASPEN OBSERVED, with pleasure, that he was not as dis-
quieted by these false starts as he would have been at one time.
On the contrary, during these days he felt a certain ebullience
and spontaneity, like an athlete warming up. He was fencing
with himself, he recognized, looking for an opening, trying
new styles and gestures. "Shadow-boxing," he said to himself,
and smiled at the aptness of the term. In his painting, he
sketched quickly with the brush, working from a neutral
palette; he blocked out tones of grass, sky, sunlight, not
caring whether the canvas was filled, and then, after an hour,
he thrust out gaily with a lighter or darker brush, fixing the
daub which could organize and animate, or disrupt and kill.
When he stood back to appraise the consequence, he found he
was pleased with either outcome, and he saw that this was
the true nature of experiment in the arts, not the decades
of pious fanfaronade on matters of form and technique to
which he had listened so attentively. And the analogy with
life was unmistakable.

ЛЛЛЛ

[Relax, Aspen. You aren't lost, you have your bearings.
Beginning with death. Death-in-life. The lucidity which leads
to madness (in spite of Camus). Failure and success. The
stone . . .

Beginning with death. Concentrating on it as the object of fear. This seems to be what everyone takes for granted. Natural enough; everyone knows what fear is. But does everyone know what death is? What does it mean to me? Leaving aside objective data or the lack of them, what does the experience of dying suggest to me? Not pain, at any rate, since the idea of dying in my sleep appalls me even more than the idea of death by violence. (Do others feel that, too? Do others wish to face it, confront it, experience it?) But if the idea of pain is not the cause of my fear, neither is the idea of loss, the loss of worldly things, pleasures, relationships, etc., the sun and sea that mean so much to Camus. I would be perfectly delighted to accept a death which would leave *me* as I am and merely change the world. But we are realists first of all, without honesty we have nothing. Hence the opposite likelihood is what frightens me; in death the world will remain the same and I will be lost. Meaning destroyed, expunged, annihilated, exterminated. *Ex nihilo ad nihilum.* Nothing: such a terrible word that the mind cannot conceive it, and we have (I have) no image of complete absence. Yet that is what my consciousness, my self, this extraordinarily complicated package of thoughts, memories, feelings, intuitions, will become. Nothing. Not as much as a millionth part of an infinite smallness. Nothing.

Item. The fear of death is the fear of personal extinction. Which we may as well call depersonalization, though the term is offensively jargonistic and reminiscent of the doctors, who probably mean something else by it anyway.

Nevertheless . . .

Neverthless, something is gained, since by looking at death under its aspect of individual depersonalization one can see more clearly why all fear, all anxiety, all terror, is derived from fear of death; there can be no other fear. This is what the neurotic person comes to know, though the process of his learning is slow and painful. But however well concealed in his subconscious the connection may be, his *Angst* in a given predicament is fear of death. Indeed, what else could it be? This is what Camus agreed to without hesitation. If we were immortal we would have no fear, for pain, suffering, humiliation, and all other ills would be endurable, once we were assured of personal continuity. At most we would suffer a minor apprehension, an animal twinge of withdrawal from the instrument of pain. (This is true even for those who are under systematic torture, since the very rationale of systematic torture is that it will be torture unto death; the victim who hastens his death in order to avoid pain does so because he knows that this pain is a part of death.) Who, being assured of immortality, would not thrust his hand with pleasure into the fire? If Sisyphus is happy, it is not because he is lucid, but because he is immortal. His lucidity is his madness.

There! A betrayal if ever one was. Camus, it pinches me. To put down these words of reversal and reversion, such conventional words, antimodern, I have gone against you, and I feel it. Yet they came; they are what I know, I, in my own realism and honesty. And I hold with you firmly on the obligation of lucidity, never think that I will abandon it. There, in the region of your greatest courage, I shall always try to follow. Can I find a reconciliation, for me, between lucidity and madness, revolt and happiness?

Item. All fear in life is fear of depersonalization.

This being so, I detect a somewhat different slant on absurdity. Nothing to contradict Camus; his description of absurdity is the bedrock, so to speak, on which all else is founded. The substance is the same. But slants are important, as well as substances; views, prospects, angles of vision; and this is something a painter is more aware of, possibly, than a writer. At any rate, it appears feasible to attempt a formulation in such terms as these. Absurdity-according-to-Camus is human consciousness rendered evanescent by the prospect of its fortuitous termination in death's nothingness, and the consequent invalidation of all meaning; more precisely, in *The Myth of Sisyphus,* absurdity is the state of tension obtaining between a lucid consciousness and meaninglessness. Absurdity-according-to-Aspen adds one element: death-in-life. That is to say, death reaching into life through the agency of fear. It is all very well for Camus to insist that fear is a constituent element of absurdity, no more gross than others, and that lucidity conquers all. It doesn't work. As a matter of fact, the entire confrontation between the lucid person and absurdity, in the descriptions Camus has given, is too static to be realistic. Absurdity is presented as an inert weight, like the stone of Sisyphus, which is countered by the individual person with an attitude of frozen scorn and rejection. But absurdity is a force, depersonalization is a force, fear is a force; and they must be met by force. The result is a contest, perpetually slipping and sliding over the same ground. Scorn and rejection are not enough.

Item. Absurdity is meaningless and valueless; but it is also dynamic.

Something more is needed, however. Precisely how does death-in-life affect us?]

ЛЛЛЛ

[I have been thinking, brooding, fantasizing, about lucidity. What I require, it seems, is more of it, a lucid view of lucidity. Mirrors in the barbershop?

Camus announces, first, the mind, with its reasonable desire to be, and the universe which unreasonably, mindlessly, irrationally, denies it. The result is meaninglessness and valuelessness, the unalterable divorce of mind and universe; in short, absurdity. Next come lucidity and revolt, the mind's self-preserving, self-integrating gestures. Revolt seems simple enough, even in the rather special meaning given to it by Camus. At one point he says, discriminating between synonyms, that revolt is rejection without renunciation; which is part of his rhetoric of agony, perfectly just and justified, I think, and leading in the end, as often as not, to a refined clarity and distinctness. Speaking in less distinct and also less rhetorical terms, what the definition appears to mean is a rejection of the mindlessness and irrationality of the universe, as manifested in the coercive negativism of death, without a renunciation of the materiality which a realistic view of the universe necessarily predicates. In other words, revolt for Camus is close to Sartre's disdainful interpretation, though the implications of Sartre's scorn may or may not be acceptable. Revolt is a disapproval of the world's quintessential irrationality, a refusal to acquiesce in it, but without any evasion (through self-delusion, magical dismissal, the intuitive leap, etc.) of the terms imposed on existence by reality. Camus insists repeatedly that the absurd man will never consent to "know" anything that he does not understand. The paradox of Tertullian, and more explicitly its modern reconstructions by Kierkegaard, Jaspers, and others, are uncompromisingly excluded, and there can be no question whatever about that.

So far, so good. Camus continues, then, by asserting that this order of revolt is not possible unless conducted in lucidity, and what he means by lucidity is consciousness of absurdity, a full and unrelenting consciousness. Only by this means may the absurd man preserve the purity of his revolt. In plain terms, he must look continually at his own foreseeable but indeterminate death, and at its "meaning" in his life, namely, that his life has no meaning. If his view wavers, if the fixity of his awareness lapses, then his revolt, by just that much, loses purpose and efficacy.

Okay. All this looks straightforward and easy, and in a

sense it is; but it doesn't work, it simply doesn't work. Life, the struggle of life, the very revolt Camus is talking about (which most of us, one way or another, have been attempting all our lives), is neither straightforward nor easy. Camus said that I oversimplified. True enough; simplification is the rule, the *raison*, of the mind, and no one who ever lived and thought could shut it off. Camus no more than others. (And here in his presence, in this room where he looks down at me from every wall, I can write in these terms only because they are the ones he would apply to himself, and has, as a matter of fact, often enough.)

For example, the use of the terms "consciousness" and "awareness." They are the fashionable terms, of course, in an era when everything is oriented to psychiatry, when human being must be considered always in its passive, objective aspects. To be "aware" of one's death, to be "conscious" of it: are these the same as looking at it, searching for it, attending to it? Are they the terms one should use in defining lucidity? The connotations are different, I should say. I don't think Camus is wrong in using terms which emphasize the passivity of the individual mind as it confronts death; on the contrary, I think he is right; but I also think his rightness takes him in a direction he probably did not foresee.

We have been admonished to study death since the beginning of recorded thought; Camus is in august company. But usually the recommendations have been made by philosophers and religious people who regarded the study of death as a spiritual exercise; that is to say, even though they may have believed that life in this world should be lived in accordance with precepts derived from the study of death, they were still primarily concerned with life as it is lived out of this world, or at least with life abstracted from the contingency of this world. Usually they have said that one must live one's life as if one were already dead, or words to that effect. The focus of their interest has been on what they considered the imperishable attributes of human personality, the "soul," which Camus, of course, denies outright, although he is not averse to using the term as a nontechnical referent for certain affective and esthetic capacities of the human (perishable) mentality. Camus declares that life must be lived solely *within* the contingency of this world, that every act of life is consequently meaningless and unpredictable, and that, even so, the man who has learned to recognize absurdity must commit these meaningless, unpredictable acts in the full and immediate acknowledgment of his own death, which is what makes the acts meaningless and unpredictable to begin with. This is lucidity; this is what gives self-consistency to revolt. But is such lucidity possible? Is there not a contradiction between the concept of acting and the concept of meaninglessness? Is an act really an act if it is completely surrounded, so to speak, by the negation of death?

Imagine Camus sitting down to write *The Stranger*. "Mother died today. Or, maybe, yesterday," etc. The words are accosting the page, a definite act is being committed. Very likely his methods of composition aren't that simple, but he began somewhere, and his beginning was, indubitably, an act. Was it committed in lucidity? Complete lucidity? By definition an act is purposive; the novel had a plan, however imprecise, the beginning entailed an ending, a middle, a series of intricate, consecutive, related acts. (I am trying to avoid the idea of strict causality.) In other words, the act of beginning the novel unavoidably invoked futurity. Perhaps Camus, the absurd man *par excellence*, could launch himself upon this exceedingly arduous, complicated course and at the same time hold firmly in his mind the idea that it was all meaningless. Maybe he could do it; maybe half a dozen other men alive on earth today could also do it. But *I* couldn't, and I am the one who, in this exigency, counts.

What I mean is that if we are to be realists, as Camus insists, we must be realistic not only about the crushing mindless force of eternity but about the ordinary capabilities of the ordinary intelligent human being. A lucidity which is limited to the saints is really not much help.

However, Camus himself has admitted that lucidity is not always possible. This was in reply to my asking whether or not one could be lucid at the moment of sexual orgasm, and then he went on to say that lucidity is unlikely during sleep, dreaming, daydreaming, etc. All this is crucial, I think, especially the connection between lucidity and sex. (And I'll leave out of account the possibility that with sufficient effort and training the individual person might attain lucidity during orgasm, or even in sleep; this would be the sort of ascetic anti-naturalism that Camus would deplore.) Camus insists (and so do I) that the objective of lucid revolt is happiness. At the same time, he would insist, I am certain, that sex is a pleasure; this is the implicit meaning of the sexual episodes in his books, and in any event it is what virtually all men believe. And pleasure is happiness. But now we know that sex cannot be lucid. Is there reason to doubt that it can be a revolt? What becomes of the notion that the absurd man, by means of his lucid revolt, will become happy? Is sex to be excluded from happiness? No. One gives the answer with a certain emphasis. (Meursault and I hold identical opinions on that score at least, and for the same reasons.) From this, two conclusions appear:

Item. Lucidity is not relentless, unceasing, or immediately necessary, as has been suggested heretofore, but intermittent. It is the product of mental and emotional energy which may, from time to time, fail. Moreover, it may be categorically precluded by certain experiential priorities, such as sex. Hence a part of lucidity is a recognition of its own limits. And is this not the same as saying that lucidity is a component of self-knowledge?

Item. The limits of lucidity are extensible. First, through the normal effort of concentration. Second and more important, through the faculties of anticipation and retrospection. Thus the act of sex may become a genuine revolt (a genuine "act") through the application of lucidity beforehand and afterward; indeed, this is the *only* way it may become a genuine act of revolt and hence a factor of absurd happiness. But this corroborates the faculties of memory and prevision. Once again the individual consciousness is seen to be functioning, in a perfectly practical manner, within the structure of time. I don't say this invalidates the concept of meaninglessness in absurdity, or even so much as chips away a tiny fragment of it; obviously, memory and prevision in themselves have no power to rationalize a mindless existence; but they do render it a little less terrifying.]

ЛЛЛЛ

[Perhaps the point is that lucidity is not *necessarily* the austere ascesis which emerges from the classical prose of *The Myth*. Lucidity, in itself, is not altogether lucid; but is variable, amorphous, and complex, even in the acute phases which one encounters, according to Camus, in artistic creation. Granting this, one then quite legitimately proceeds to play with the idea a bit, to push it around and see what happens. And the first question that occurs to me is: what, functionally speaking, is lucidity?

Looking at death, I have said. But looking how? That is important, too. If one adopts an objective view of one's own demise as an historical event possessing the matter-of-factness and localization of other historical events; if, in other words, one views one's own death in the same terms that one applies to the deaths of others, then this is an exercise in abstraction resulting in abstract knowledge. But Camus has said repeatedly

that this is not what he has in mind. In the first place, the
images of lucidity which appear throughout his work, for
example Meursault's "dark wind" blowing from the future,
invariably denote affective knowledge, something felt and
suffered. In the second place, Camus has explicitly denied the
usefulness of reason and abstract knowledge, saying that since
we cannot *know* everything, i.e., the answers to ultimate
questions, then all knowledge is suspect and inefficacious. (This
is too sweeping a rejection, of course, and he modifies it
elsewhere; but in respect to lucidity the point is valid.) In
short, lucidity is, for Camus, the immediate felt presence of
death shadowing all our acts, the taste of death in the mouth,
the brine of death in the veins. And obviously we must agree
that this is the only kind of lucidity which can be effectual in
the absurd life as Camus conceives it.

But again, is it possible? The doctors say no; they say the
ordinary man, in the interest of sanity, must put his own
death out of his mind, and that even the person who is not
ordinary must contemplate his own death at an abstract remove, as if, so to speak, it were going to happen to somebody
else. For once I'm inclined to agree with the doctors. Suppose
there are a few people, Camus among them, who can retain
their lucidity in the perpetual seizure of death, what about *me*?
If I had not thought, if I had not believed profoundly, that
Camus was fundamentally concerned about me in everything
he has written, I should never have been attracted to his work
in the first place.

Soldiers at the active salient of the front, in the midst of
virtually ceaseless artillery barrage and under constant aerial
bombardment, those who have already been written off at the
headquarters fifteen miles away, still believe, individually, in
their luck. Condemned criminals in the death cells are convinced until the end that their appeals will be granted. As for
me, when the fever of death is upon me, as it is far too often
for my self-possession and as it has been at close intervals ever

since that terribly unforgettable night when I first started upright in my bed, clutching my unripe body in the dark, then I have very little lucidity at all. Then it is a question of hysteria, quaking, and blindness.

Item. We come round again, by a different route, to the same point: the limit of lucidity. Taking, as we must, a realistic view of human capability, we conclude that lucidity is limited by the degree of tension which the individual consciousness can support. A pure, perfect lucidity will destroy itself, leaving its opposite in its place: madness. Thus lucidity itself is a tension, an emotional advance and withdrawal, a continually tentative and renewed approach toward the full affective realization of death, prosecuted under the perpetual risk of insanity.]

ЛЛЛЛ

[Getting back to the idea of depersonalization, clearly this is the factor of death which no lucidity, as I have come to understand it, can withstand for long; at least not for long at one time. (No lucidity? Do I speak for the world? I, too, speak for myself. But how I fear, distrust, uniqueness, which reminds me of loneliness. Hence this public manner, this expository, expostulatory manner, this absolutely ridiculous manner!)

And it seems to me at this point that the idea of lucidity has been made both stronger and weaker by what I have done. Stronger, because it is less stiff, brittle, frangible. Weaker, because I have taken from it some of the transcendent . . . no, wrong word: some of the overriding, overseeing, almost supervisory power given to it by Camus. And yet I agree with him perfectly that without lucidity nothing is possible, nothing. I agree with him, or with his implication, that lucidity is his grandest conception. To restore it, what must be done? Isn't it possible that, instead of tinkering further with the concept of lucidity, I should try to redirect it toward a new, or additional, object?

Here the idea of depersonalization helps, I think. Depersonalization in death is an ultimate depersonalization, the extirpation of the person, the erasure of the person. But everyone knows that depersonalization is also a factor of life; it is all around us; we feel it every day acting upon us in a thousand ways. Not ultimate depersonalization, not total obliteration of the person, but a constant abrading and restriction of the person; it amounts to a depersonalization which is less than ultimate, but not much less. The question is, can lucidity, directed toward this less-than-ultimate depersonalization, withstand it? And the answer: yes. Because this depersonalization is a factor of life, not a factor of death.

An example; the first that comes to mind. A supermarket, relative to the old-fashioned general store, is a depersonalizing instrumentality. The individual person in a supermarket, whether employee or client, is treated in such a manner, predicated in such a manner, that his being as a person is, although not destroyed, nevertheless reduced, suppressed, distorted, degraded, disabled, etc. There can be no doubt of this, even though the supermarket is not the most vicious of the depersonalizing forces in life and even though few people have suffered depersonalization in supermarkets to the extent of a genuine loss of identity; other depersonalizing forces in life are greater, and all of them taken together are very great, quite great enough to decimate the identities of entire masses of people. But the point is that the lucidity of the lucid person can withstand the supermarket precisely because the supermarket is a depersonalizing force, not in death, but explicitly in life. The supermarket dispenses the necessities of life; it itself has been made necessary by the process of life, which multiplies persons until new and more effective means for distributing goods are required. (Even here in France, where resistance to depersonalization is stronger than elsewhere, the supermarket has made a beginning; so I hear in the kitchen.) Nor can it properly be said, I think, that the supermarket is a concealed or indirect agency of death, working in the disguise of life, such as a parasitical organism which supports its own life by destroying the life on which it feeds. This is a common figure of speech used by those who dislike supermarkets, but it seems to me inaccurate. The supermarket really is just a supermarket: an inevitable phase in social morphology, in itself scarcely existent, a sort of managerial fiction. On the other hand, there can be no question about its depersonalizing influence.

Does this require Camus to alter anything he has said in his theory of the absurd? Not at all. Death remains the supreme depersonalizing factor, the supreme creator of supreme meaninglessness. This absurdity is irreducible. On the other hand, the depersonalizing forces of life are all, at least in theory, amenable to change, and in consequence the meaninglessness which derives from them is subsidiary and, so to speak, contingent. The absurdity of death is fundamental. The absurdity of life is derivative, but still important. Important because we, as we have said, are realists and practical men, and we recognize that the individual person who makes a gesture of lucid revolt against the subsidiary depersonalizing forces of life can expect to produce no greater an external effect than the person who makes a gesture of lucid revolt against the supreme depersonalizing force of death. His plight is *virtually* the same in both cases, but with one difference: since depersonalization in life still leaves the existential self-identification of the person intact, lucidity can hold it in view more constantly and less dangerously than is the case with the affective image of death.

Item. Death-in-life is the tyranny against which lucidity may commit the genuine act of revolt, not only without a loss of strength, but with a probable gain. Lucidity may hold death-in-life safely in view, without vertigo, without the blurring of its own power. This strengthened lucidity may then be applied to death and fundamental absurdity more intensely and perhaps more protractedly, and with less risk of devastation.]

⊓⊔⊓⊔⊓

FOR YEARS Aspen had not known fatigue, but only the stung mind's insomnia. Now he was tired. As he lay in his cot at night, before he switched off his lamp, he looked around his walls at the sketches of his friend. Yes, some were stony all right, no doubt of it; and his eyes went to his stone, which occupied a position of relative majesty upon the stove. A good solid stone; perhaps one would not wish to stray far from it. Yet it was the fluidity and simplicity of the stone that attracted him now, and he saw, or thought he saw, as he glanced back to the sketches, that he had captured it in a few of them. As for the canvases he had done lately, the olive-colored hayfields threaded with brown sunlight, one might, he thought, if one came upon them unexpectedly, be tempted to call them serene. "Booker T. Braque himself," he muttered, naming the imaginary painter whom he had invented to represent academicism and docility. He smiled, turned out his light, and went to sleep.

⊓⊔⊓⊔⊓

[Depersonalization in life occurs in so many ways that perhaps I am wasting my time to classify them; but that is the way the mind works. Two main categories have appeared to me, and

I may as well put them on paper, as a means of clearing the boards, so to speak. (Expression as evacuation; cf. Sean Joyce.) The first category, which was represented by my supermarket, is simple enough; I mean the whole concatenation of destructive pressures bearing upon the individual consciousness from its human environment: social, political, commercial, academic, and so on; the forms are nearly endless. The most obvious form, however, is the state. In *The Rebel*, without pretending to tell the whole story, Camus has described the way in which the modern state has become a superperson through a sort of metaphysical overthrow or debasement of the idea of a superpersonal deity. Perhaps his analysis is not entirely correct, perhaps no one's analysis is entirely correct; this seems to me the kind of all-encompassing historical movement that can never be understood; nevertheless the fact of the superpersonal state is evident. The superpersonal state becomes the superperson, and there isn't anyone alive, I imagine, who isn't aware of the superperson every day of his existence. Against the superperson, the person is literally nothing: a no-thing. The superperson, with mindless tyranny, destroys the person out of hand, turning him into an abstraction, a token, a statistical unit of labor, consumption, revenue, or the like. The other superpersons, the "corporate personalities" of commercial and institutional life, do precisely the same thing. All this superpersonal force bears down upon the individual person with one purpose: to inform him that he does not exist and that he has no claim to existence. He has sinned simply by being born. Useless to stand there gaping, repeating, "But it's me, me, can't you understand?" The superperson understands nothing; has no ears, no heart, and above all no mind. It is unreachable, unpropitiable. Its busy factotum, himself mindless, is the advertising man, whose declared purpose is the substitution of superpersonal determinism for individual will, using any and all means, including deceit, including even "subliminal" manipulation. What, short

of death, could be more destructive? This is a critical depersonalization, and its result in the person is a general neurosis
which I call the Babylonian Neurosis.

In using the term "neurosis," however, I have in mind something not quite coincidental with clinical usage; something
larger, something both more beautiful and more ugly, something more nearly associated with the higher intellectual and
volitional centers than with the instincts; in short, something
which requires a moral understanding, something tragic.

Another demurrer. Apologists for collectivism and cor-
poratism, by no means limited to the Marxists, often say that
the concept of the superperson is as old as humanity itself,
that it is the logical and necessary basis for social organization, and that modern life, in submitting so completely, after
a brief fling at individualism, to the effacing tyranny of the
superperson, is seeking a return to a more protected mode
of existence. The case is open to historical argument, I should
say, but it would be pointless. Who cares? Whether it is
an early or a late invention, whether it was born in Athens or
Geneva, the human personality is present and it is ours. Part
of lucidity, the essential part, as Camus says, is the preserva-
tion of both terms in the absurd relationship, the meaningless
universe and the individual consciousness. Actual suicide destroys the latter term, thus destroying lucidity; philosophical
suicide, the "existential leap," the intuitive reliance on hypothetical explanations, destroys the former term, with equal
results for lucidity. To these I would add a third, the
collective suicide, the immersion of the living self in a worldly
fiction of superpersonality, which destroys both terms together.

My second category is less clear; that is to say, it is a
category of depersonalization in life which appears to connect
with depersonalization in death, and the line between is not
distinct, at least not to me. Nevertheless, there is a category
of depersonalizing experience which derives from the objec-

tive universe considered as eternity, and which appears to be apart from the depersonalizing experience of individual death. The acknowledgment of the stars, the sea, etc. The contemplation of evolution, etc. The amplitudes of infinitesimal existences, etc. All magnitudes, in fact; all realities which, for reasons of simple immeasurability, surpass the understanding. Customarily people speak of the experience of eternity as an apprehension of the death of the species, the works of mankind passing out of existence as the stars and planets tread their unending orbits; and in this sense it is clearly a part of depersonalization in death. But I think it is also true that people experience eternity from life itself, from the immensity of life. There are equally good "reasons" to suppose the species will go on forever, or that it will end tomorrow. The experience of the supposition is the experience of the *living* nullity of individual existence in the radical relativity of sheer dimension. And I call the neurosis which it produces in the individual person the Jewish Neurosis.

It is worth noticing that the term "category," meaning a subjective mode or organization for experience, is precisely applicable here. From a point of vantage outside experience, all depersonalization would be the same and would be indistinguishable from the potato blight or an avalanche in Switzerland. It is also worth noticing that categories, whether or not they are fixed according to anything like a genuine a priori or "racially unconscious" order, nevertheless do tend to fall into recognizable patterns; the Jewish Neurosis and the Babylonian Neurosis conform roughly to the categories which Camus denotes by the concepts of God and history, the absolutes of faith and the absolutes of determinism, metaphysical revolt and political revolt, etc.

Item. The neurotic condition of mankind is a natural response to depersonalization; since depersonalization in death is an inalterable factor, and since we cannot assume that there has been an increase in lucidity, the intensification of the neurotic condition of mankind in the modern era must be a result of an intensified depersonalization in life. This is simply a restatement in other terms of what I have already said.]

⊓⊔⊓⊔

[If the neuroses which result from depersonalization in life are called the Jewish Neurosis and the Babylonian Neurosis, then what is the neurosis that results from an apprehension of depersonalization in death? Naturally, the Christian Neurosis.]

⊓⊔⊓⊔

[Of course, what I have been trying to get at, during these weeks, has been a conception or image of revolt which would be more useful, more serviceable, to someone in my circumstances than the image of the strong, silent, Humphrey Bogartian rebel that emerges from most of the remarks of Camus. No criticism implied. Mr. Bogart was the secret idol of a whole generation of American artists and intellectuals, and Camus comes very near to embodying that ideal; the two even resemble one another in appearance. But most of these same artists and intellectuals have been forced to recognize, in their personal lives, that they are far from strong and silent, far from Bogartian, but instead hyperalgesic, hyperesthetic, hypertrophied in virtually every respect, and, from the standpoint of physical and moral evolution, ineffectual representatives of the species. To such persons, what kind of revolt is possible and useful?

Tonight is fiercely hot. More like America than France. Now that the end is near, summer has put aside her gentle ways, so to speak, and turned into the Amazon that we half suspected and feared all along. This room might as well be in the tropics. In fact, only a small effort of imagination is required to transport it; by squinting my ears a trifle I can hear, beyond the shutters, street noises from Léopoldville, necrotic whisperings, a jackal in the distance. Singularly, my painting was quickened. This afternoon I slashed at the canvas more vigorously than ever, sweating and striving like a mired ox, and was vastly contented, I must say, with the result: a new tone of blue density and virility in the browns and ochers; the marching willows in their sequacious idiocy. Now I sit in my ease. The perspiration grows on me like a coat of fur. I am glossy and handsome.

But is the rebel of Camus strong and silent? Not really; that is a superficial impression, however purposively it may have been created. And I think Camus would perhaps approve, no doubt with a sidelong glance, my Babylonian, Jewish, and Christian Neuroses, because he could very easily counter them with his concept of Hellenic salubrity; the idea of limits, the idea of a sensible, justifiable, admissible perspective, above all the idea of the dialogue, upon which he banks so heavily. Curiously, I do not recall the name Aristotle being once invoked in the novels and essays. On the contrary, the explicit references are to the Platonic and Neo-Platonic conventions, amalgamated mythopoetically with vague Homeric and Pindaric sentiments; but the center, the *locus*, it seems to me, is the Nicomachean Ethics. In this, of course, Camus is close to every other Western artist and intellectual since Cicero, drawn poetically to the Socratic style and spirit, drawn intellectually to the Aristotelian mode of aggressive inquiry, with the result that the Hellenic extravaganza, to which Camus subscribes himself without reservation, is one of the three or four most significant historical fictions ever invented.

Tonight these matters seem forceful, cogent, and close at hand. I am myself a Camusan rebel; with the rest I, too, stake my fortunes at Salamis, *against* Babylon and all that it entails. This is an active struggle, by no means silent, and a genuine revolt, the new against the old, if not (remembering Camus) a renunciation, then at least, without compromise, a denunciation. We are *against*. We say it boldly, we say it coldly and angrily: the tyranny of the encroaching order is intolerable. Against it, we shall preserve this little region, this soul, this dying and juvenescent Greece.

As to the manner of my revolt, I must go beyond Camus; or rather, not beyond, since I would lack the genius to do so, but through: that is, I must readjust his vision to my eyes. And since depersonalization in life, the erosion and repression of the person by the superpersonal forces of life, is the aspect of absurdity to which I can give my lucid attention most successfully, I find I am able to say, simply and without further circumvention, that my act of revolt must be a continual fortifying and rebuilding of my person in life. Death and the supreme absurdity will engage my heed during my moments of heightened lucidity and courage, and then I, too, will submit myself to the regimen of contemplative ferocity, the static contest of the willed and the unwilled. In these moments my strength will be tested and, with luck, purified. But my strength itself must derive rather from the continual, lived struggle with life, the struggle to create myself and become a person, to reconstitute myself in the face of the relentless abrasions of life. In this struggle, I perform in the prescribed negative manner, disclaiming what I cannot deny, resisting what I cannot refuse, opposing what I cannot overcome; but I seek continually to perform also in an affirmative manner, creating myself, enriching my person, enlarging the ground of my opponency. Just as the greater confrontation with death is an inevitable failure, so this lesser confrontation also fails; but in an altered sense. Failure here is the person's inability to achieve himself wholly; no whole person has ever been known on earth; nor will be, given absurdity. But neither is the person, in life, ever completely destroyed; even in madness a modicum remains.

Item. Genuine revolt against depersonalization is personalization; in life, possible; in death, not.]

ЛЛЛЛ

[Enough of items, I imagine. You can't itemize reality, not in man's time, but only offer samples; which is what my items really were. Discrete views, shots in the dark. (But at least I was hunting the real beast. Elsewhere the marksmen have not interrupted their target practice.)

Rebelling against the absurdity of existence, striving toward the realization of my person, knowing that self-realization can never be more than seriously imperfect, what means do I choose? The means choose me; they are what I am. I think the description and elaboration of epistemological hypotheses could be almost endless; the marksmen have been at it for centuries, after all. The fact is, the pragmatic fact, that the human mentality, taken as a whole, taken, in other words, as any combination of apperceptive, affective, rational, and volitional faculties you choose, is a marvelous machine for turning experience into personality; and this is its end. That is what I insist on, for myself, and let the mechanism be the concern of others. The end, the objective, the purpose is the progressive realization of the person. If these self-realizing procedures issue also in acts which occur in the external world, these acts are by-products, meaningless in themselves; given the conditions of absurdity, they must be meaningless. And they must be useless, *except* as they in turn become the fodder, so to speak, the *materia experientia,* of succeeding efforts of self-realization. (From that "except" issue momentous consequences, of course.)

Is self-realization what the Greeks meant by self-knowledge? The meaning may be close; but there is a semantic difficulty. Knowledge, in the positivistic sense, is ultimately valueless, as Camus has insisted, and consequently self-realization cannot consist of exercises in analysis. On the contrary, when we objectify ourselves, we lend ourselves to the forces of depersonalization, thus producing the opposite effect from that for which we strive. Self-realization is a means of realizing the person, becoming the person, and in this (older) sense we do "know" ourselves, as we say that we "know" a certain woman; we perceive ourselves directly and immediately.

All that need be said, really, about the epistemological mechanism is that consciousness, so far as it is anything more than perception on an animal level, is imaginative, and that experience is memorable only in terms of metaphor. These are an artist's terms, of course, and other people might not accept them. The scientist would say that he "hypothecates" and "extemporizes inductively," etc. Well, what difference does it make? Any attempt to define the personality in terms of faculties seems to me ultimately fruitless because it is ultimately unverifiable, like all subjective matters. Then is there any definition of personality? Is there any definition of anything? At any rate, there are "working definitions," which are perhaps sufficient. A working definition of personality: immense, fluid congeries of experience, mnemonically constituted and metaphorically integrated.

Whew!]

⊓⊔⊓⊔

[Success and failure, then. Meursault achieved lucidity too late to make his act of revolt successful in more than a painfully limited sense; at least, that appears to be a provisional, midway interpretation, though one is certain that much more remains to be said. Camus suggested that, in contrast, my moment of revolt was successful and hence lucid. At the time the idea seemed strange enough to be shocking; certainly there was no feeling of success. Yet the elements of lucidity were there: chiefly anger, violent anger; and if it was a suppressed and misdirected anger which turned instantaneously into fear (of reprisal), well, I was aware of that, too. My hysteria, my flight, were failures only when considered in the most conventional way, to which I had, of course, been deeply conditioned. I ran away. Hence no feeling of success. But the success lay in the imperceptible enlargement and enrichment of myself that accrued from the memory of the fear and anger, constituted within me as a specific, if not unique, metaphor of pines-wall-street-streetlight-woman-wind.]

⊓⊔⊓⊔

[In any event, success is limited. What is Camus talking about? He is talking about getting by, he is talking about survival, he is talking about a minimal accomplishment. Nothing more, in the face of absurdity. And absurdity is not only death, not only death-in-life, but . . . yes, the point comes clearer now:

absurdity, the most immediate and compelling aspect of absurdity, is *in ourselves.* This is the thing to hit on. Personal failure, misjudgment, ignorance, cowardice, suffering, everything that is called fallibility, even murder! We are like Tarrou in *The Plague,* who is searching for sainthood but finds he cannot elude the quintessential human disqualification, complicity in the deaths of others. It is built in, it is part of being born. And my lucidity, imperfect as it was, shredded by guilt and shame that had been heaped on me by others, then by myself, as if any of us were guilty, as if any of us were anything but innocent of this monstrous crime which resounds through the universe! . . . my lucidity, nevertheless, recognized the irreducible justice of my anger, the irreducible integrity of my existence, and this kept me alive all those black years.]

ЛЛЛЛ

[A limited success is not likely to elicit a "feeling of success." What elation, what triumph in these circumstances? The idea is laughable. But it is just this laugh which Camus converts to scorn.]

ЛЛЛЛ

[My thoughts return, tonight, to the idea of time. Is it important, the idea, important for *us?* Don't know. But if the personality is held to be a structure of memory, then the past, at any rate, is important. In a completely real sense, we live *in* it as well as *on* it. Yet without hope. Like a widower who cannot be reconciled to the loss of his wife and sinks into an endless and despairing reverie? No, that would be to escape, quite literally, into the past, and hence is incompatible with lucidity, which permits no escape. Then perhaps it is more like a mountain climber who remembers what he has learned on the gentler slopes below as he picks his way up the palisades of the midjourney. Or who remembers what he has learned in a fall as he resumes his climb.

My difficulty, I expect, is that I cannot believe in the reality of the present moment. This is shocking, after Camus; yet if I cannot, I cannot. Is it as radical a departure from Camus as it seems? Does he say that the only reality is the present, does he go that far? I think his commentators are the ones who do that for him. It is possible to live in time without living in history. Not only possible but necessary, just as it is necessary to live in meaninglessness without living in derangement. And because prevision is only memory inverted, the corollary is this: it is possible to live in expectation without living in hope.

Aside from the conundrum contained in the self-evident proposition that the present moment is infinitely divisible, aren't we all perfectly aware that the moment does not exist, that what we call the present is the flux itself, the past launching itself upon the future? Our minds and bodies are innately attuned to action, to launching. We launch ourselves upon the sea of the possible person. The point is to do it in the manner of a swimmer, not in the manner of a suicide.

Memory and expectation, not to be confused with history and hope. Happiness has no present, lucidity no rest. Existence is without value or values. Yet it is not, because of this, necessarily devoid of order.]

⊓⊔⊓⊔⊓

[But if existence is ordered, does it not have at least an esthetic value?]

⊓⊔⊓⊔⊓

[Life for art's sake. Is this, in axiom, the purport of Camus? !?!?!?!

Dangerous ground.]

⊓⊔⊓⊔⊓

AT THE end of summer, Aspen's spirit of enterprise gave out. He did nothing; he was in the dumps. Only one new thought occurred to him: for the first time, in a depressed cycle, he had not retired exclusively to his room. He sat much of the time in a corner of the kitchen, fascinated by the spectacle of an apple paring, charmed by the music of the *potage*. Outdoors, it rained; the light was green. Not Aspen's idea of a good color. "Doesn't move," he explained, cheerfully enough, to the kitchen girl. "Doesn't do much of anything, really. Just clots." The girl, who was fifty-three years old and modestly arthritic, clucked sympathetically.

Aspen was wondering when Camus would come back.

ЛЛЛЛ

[Floundering. Floundering. Halibuting. I was. Questions of value: over my head. Camus says clearly enough that the value is life. A sensible, demonstrable, attractive, agreeable view. And is it necessary to proceed from the subjective to the objective, that crossing of the Rubicon? Not now; not for me. Never, for that matter, if the objective means . . . well, if it means anything too damned *large*. We are, I repeat, talking about a way, *one* way; we are making a start; we are concerned with what we understand, nothing more.

We must be bold, that goes without saying. But this does not mean that we cannot permit ourselves the indulgence of being careful, too.

Still and all . . .

Still and all I am not satisfied; not wholly, not sufficiently. Something gnaws away. Something on that windy night demands a further acknowledgment. But what is it? Haven't we been over them all? Time? History? Freedom? Justice? Nature? Love?]

ЛЛЛЛ

[*Love ! ! !*]

part four

꟱꟱꟱

CAMUS AND Aspen traveled south in November. The autumn was foul that year, damp and cold for weeks at a time; everyone was depressed. But the season was no better on the coast than it had been inland, and, in any event, Camus had not sought to evade the weather. "This is November, this is Europe," he had said, and shrugged. He had business with a friend, he explained, a friend who would put them up; and he would be glad of Aspen's company. Aspen was delighted, of course, and flattered. He offered to drive them both down from Paris.

"Drive?"

"I've bought a car."

"A car? How extraordinary!"

Aspen flushed with pleasure. The car was, in fact, such an advance in his mobility and freedom that he found himself still incredulous; each morning he ran out to see if it was really there. As he touched it, gently and tentatively, his eyes softened. It was an Alfa Giuletta, black and new, as tight and beautiful as a new box of paints; and the two, Aspen and Camus, were close and comfortable as they traveled south through the rain.

Camus was obviously pleased with his friend's progress. And pleased with the Alfa, too; he tried everything, switched on the map light, pushed in the cigarette lighter, adjusted his seat, looked in the back and under the dash. For some time, as they drove, they talked about matters of carburetion, gear ratios, displacement, the advantages and disadvantages of overhead cams; matters which, in truth, were still largely cryptic to Aspen; and he greatly admired the erudition of Camus, who expounded at length on the new disk brakes which had recently appeared on some models. "Much easier to cool," he said, "and then, of course, they can be set inboard, especially on the rear where you need the extra flexibility of suspension." But at length the conversation flagged.

After several false starts, Aspen inquired about the friend they were on their way to visit.

"Fellow named D'Arrast."

"That's an odd name."

"Think so?"

"Well, perhaps not. Have you known him long?"

"Four or five years. Maybe longer."

"I see. Is he a close friend?"

"Hard to say, actually."

Camus had a way of shutting off topics he did not care to discuss. Nevertheless, Aspen attempted one further question: "Does he speak English?"

"Oh, yes. If you wish him to."

They drove in silence, then, admiring the glistening fields on either hand, while Aspen considered the possibly mystifying quality of his friend's last remark.

⎍⎍⎍

[An unusual place, beyond a doubt. We arrived a few hours ago, after dark, though Camus knew the way perfectly. High above the sea; looking toward Africa through bare limbs of what appears, improbably, to be a grove of dead cottonwoods; off a bit from town, though I can see the last three lights of the esplanade at the extreme lower left of my window. The limbs of the trees clatter a good deal in the wind. A big house, and I suppose at one time a wealthy man's house, but now exceedingly shabby, gone to ruin; yet probably not more than twenty-five or thirty years old. I noticed, as we came in, patches where the outside stucco has peeled away. Inside, rather dirty and quite bare; cold tile floors, or hardwood glazed with stained and flaking varnish. The window frames are half-rotten and leaky, permitting the wind to come through and rattle the venetian blinds. Furniture chiefly aluminum, rattan, cedar, etc., summer furniture and quite worn; except for the beds, which are, mine at any rate, good old four-posters, splendid for sleeping. In fact, the place has the air of being used primarily for hibernation.

D'Arrast is dark and somewhat burly, taciturn, and I should say intelligent. Bearish perhaps, or is that simply an association with hibernating? At any rate, he greeted us unsmilingly, but with a good handshake, and then cooked a late dinner for us, sausages simmered in wine, an omelet and salad, very good indeed. He cooked it all himself, although he has a girl here, extremely attractive to me, named Dora; not his wife, obviously, but I'm uncertain yet what their relationship may be. She is small and slight, a small serious face, dark brown hair which is rather thick, small hands, small teeth, small, small, small: it seems, unexpectedly, a rather beautiful word, meaning delicate but not fragile, if there can be such a distinction. She said practically nothing. She wore a suede belted jacket with the collar turned up in back. No make-up. Smoked many cigarettes and has a bad cough.

I hope she won't mind being sketched.

All my things are here, then, the stone, the paints, etc., here in this unlikeliest of places. Which is simply a way of saying that *I* am here. Strange, I ought to be frightened, but I'm not; perhaps tomorrow. As for Camus, he seems quieter, something on his mind, I expect; probably something to do with D'Arrast, though I still don't know what that connection is, either. In all events, Camus is unwilling to resume our former discussions, which is a disappointment. But no doubt everything will change in a day or two.

The Alfa is parked halfway in one arch of a dilapidated loggia out back, along with rusted lawnmowers and wheelbarrows. I'd rather have gotten her completely covered. Too damn many seagulls around here.]

⊓⊔⊓⊔

A WRITER is defenseless against his friends. His critics, his readers, his editors may be fended off; but his friends will eat him alive. So Camus protested. "Those others," he said, waving his hand, "I expect them to harp away on the old themes. But you? Have an ounce of pity, for Pete's sake."

"No question of pity whatever," D'Arrast said.

"As you yourself would be the first to maintain," Aspen added.

They were sitting in a large room where the floor was tiled in patterns of blue and white; damp sand gritted under their shoes. Beyond the windows was a balcony, now littered with broken twigs and leaves. The sky was gray; the sea smelled of kerosene, and the wind was cold and sharp. The gulls shook and slithered in the gale. Inside, radiators at either end of the room hissed steadily.

"Still, you can't blame me for being tired."

"Of course not. We're all tired." D'Arrast was whittling a wooden match with a large jackknife.

Aspen, who was sketching gulls rapidly in the pages of a book by Paul Morand, squinted against the light of the window. "But can you expect us to believe," he asked, "that the ideas to which you have devoted your life are unimportant to you?"

"It is just their importance that has made me tired." Camus pinched the thin part of his nose between his thumb and forefinger. "Do you know, I feel more like Meursault now than I did when I wrote the book?"

"Really," D'Arrast responded abruptly. "Then you ought to be able to tell us what he was thinking."

"Well, I'm not—"

"Seriously. Aspen was saying a while ago that Meursault achieved lucidity only at the end of the book, and that in consequence none of his prior actions was an action in the proper sense. And you seemed to agree with him."

"Seemed, perhaps . . ."

"You are thinking of the four shots?"

"Of course."

Aspen turned a page of his book. "I didn't mean to suggest that the four shots had not been in my mind, too. They must be in every reader's mind, for that matter; they are the most enigmatic point in the book. They are so damned enigmatic that many people must just throw up their hands. Or, what's worse, find themselves experiencing a certain fellow feeling with the magistrate in his despair over Meursault's inability to account for them."

"What's so bad about that?"

"Well, most people don't care much for the magistrate, I imagine; at least I don't. One of a type with the priest, isn't he? Lost in the kind of 'nostalgia' that is described so disdainfully in *The Myth of Sisyphus*?"

"Yes, superficially. Most of what the magistrate says is wrong and conventional. But, in the first place, I don't have the same impression of disdain in *The Myth* as you do; on the contrary, I think the nostalgia Camus is talking about there is something quite human and understandable, even something beautiful in many of its historical manifestations. Actually, the disdain, if you can call it that, seems to me more self-directed, in a sense: Camus seems almost disdainful of himself for his own need to break with nostalgia, and to try to create beauty on another, less acceptable, less deeply rooted base. As for the magistrate, even Meursault recognizes his human capacities. It seems to me that as you consider him more and more closely, he becomes less and less the stereotype of the magistrate. As a matter of fact, the further you work your way into the world of the novel, the more you see that the secondary characters are only superficially types. When you are truly inside the novel, the surface patterns of symbol and allegory are seen to be . . . well, not exactly abstractions, but something unintelligible without the depth of human and ambiguous meaning beneath them. Like the facets of a cut gem, perhaps, which take their beauty only from the interior remoteness. At any rate, I don't see why anyone should feel disturbed for sympathizing with any of the people in the book."

"Even the judge?" Camus asked.

"Naturally, one despises judges; that goes without saying. But in the book nothing is said to indicate that the judge behaves incorrectly, or that he takes any relish in his work. And at one point Meursault even says that the judge speaks to him with an air of 'cordiality.' "

"That's true," Aspen said. "And I remember thinking long ago that even the Robot Woman is not as shallow and easy to interpret as she appears to be at first."

After a moment's silence, D'Arrast said: "Come, Camus, what about those four shots? Let us put you on the spot."

"I'm damned if I'll let you put me on the spot; you or anyone. I have a perfect right as an artist, you know, to refuse."

"I was thinking of your obligation as a friend."

"Horsepiddle." Camus turned toward Aspen. "You've been thinking about them, you say, why don't you tell us what the four shots mean?"

Aspen sniffed, and began to make studious antlers on his page. "Okay, if you like. Though I didn't say I had anything to offer . . . Perhaps a place to start, or to start again, is with formal questions. At least I'm certain I am not the only reader who has been struck by the tidiness of the book's two divisions or who has tried to discover parallels between them. At one point I thought perhaps the book moved forward and backward, in equal and balanced steps, from the central episode, which was the shot that killed the Arab; then it would be like decussate leaves branching from a single stem. I'm not so sure now, though. It doesn't quite work out. Even so, one can't put out of one's mind the many evident equivalences between the two divisions; the trial in the second part, for instance, is a more elaborate repetition of the scene in the first part when Meursault is faced, across his mother's coffin, by her friends from the 'home' who have come to sit up with the body: he himself speaks of them as jurors. The questioning by the magistrate in the second part is an enlargement of the interview with the warden in the first part. There are hundreds . . . well, dozens of repeated images: for example, the cry of Salamano's dog which, in the first part, Meursault hears rising from the stairwell of his apartment house, and then, in the second part, his comparison of his own imprisonment with that of a man who is trapped in a hollow tree trunk, able to see nothing but a small disk of sky overhead. Remarkably beautiful, that. Just the kind of unstated, delitescent echo painters are always striving for, and damn seldom achieve." He turned to Dora: "I say, do you mind if I sketch you?"

She was sitting apart from the others, staring out the window with her chin propped in her hand. She seemed startled by Aspen's question. "No, no," she said over her shoulder, "go ahead."

Aspen turned a page and began rapid strokes with his felt pen. "The chief parallel in the two divisions of the book is obviously the two endings, I'd say, which is why my other idea of a form branching in two directions from the center doesn't hold up. (Though it doesn't altogether fall down, either.) At the end of the second part, which is the end of the novel, of course, Meursault experiences an access of genuine lucidity after his outburst against the priest, which we have called, for this reason, his one act of genuine revolt. At the end of the first part, he experiences a somewhat similar access of lucidity, whether genuine or not remains to be seen; he speaks of the way the fierce heat and blinding light suddenly diminish after he has fired the first shot at the Arab, leaving him, presumably, with a clearer mind."

"Yes, but if that is the case," D'Arrast interposed, "then something is wrong with your parallel. I mean that if the first shot at the Arab, committed in blind rage and radical nonlucidity, is what brings on the lucidity of the first part, and if the outburst against the priest is what brings it on in the second part, then the outburst against the priest cannot itself be the genuine act of revolt; at least not if the parallel is exact."

"I saw that coming, and I agree. Perhaps the parallel is not exact. Or perhaps we, I, must change the scheme somewhat. Is it fair to say that, at the end, Meursault's lucidity is the result of his outburst against the priest, and that his act of genuine revolt is the outcome of his lucidity? That's the logical order, at any rate, following the prescripts laid down in *The Myth;* and, of course, it means that Meursault's act of genuine revolt must be his going to his execution, which is the only act that follows his lucidity."

"How in the world can going to one's own execution be a revolt?"

"Look at it this way: he goes unwillingly but happily. In the circumstances, which are those of all of us, he can do nothing to avoid his death; he has given up hope of escape or reprieve, which is to say that he has become lucid. But he does not acquiesce. The point is made somewhere that most criminals who are condemned to execution end by asking forgiveness and even by complying, horribly and insanely, in their own death sentence. This is something that Meursault resolutely rejects. He even wishes for a mob to jeer at him as the blade descends, signifying his final and unalterable spirit of opposition. That is revolt in its purest form, isn't it? And, of course, it is what gives him his happiness." Aspen looked toward Camus.

"Go on," Camus said, shifting in his chair and crossing his legs, as if to indicate he had nothing further to say.

Aspen turned to a fresh page in his book, and looked back again to Dora. "Then the problem seems to be," he said, "primarily with the ending of the first part. Here we have a period of lucidity, however brief, which is brought on by an act of rage. And it is worth noting that rage is the efficient agent in both ca—"

"But elsewhere Camus has said that not rage but indignation is the prelude to lucidity. There *is* a difference."

"Yes, I agree that that is important. It might be a way to explain the four shots. Let's say that Meursault, in his metaphysical rage, commits an act of rebellion, the shooting of the Arab, which is ineffectual and which has been rendered ineffectual by the very blindness of his rage itself. In his moment of lucidity he recognizes this, recognizes everything; and then he fires the four additional shots by way of admitting his own failure, the failure of blind rage to do the work of lucid indignation. Is that possible?"

"Possible, but not likely, I'd say. At least if that were the case, then there'd be no need for the second half of the book. Meursault would already have learned all he needed to know."

"Then is it possible, going even further, that Meursault fires the additional shots precisely in order to enforce his own criminality, which he now recognizes? Is it possible that he wishes to make his guilt totally unpardonable?"

"Not at all. The very essence of Meursault is his avowal of his own eternal innocence."

"His own and everyone's." Aspen put down his pen and flexed his fingers. "Perhaps the four shots aren't really so enigmatic, then. What can they be but what they seem, simple despair? Meursault's moment of lucidity, which is, we know, extremely brief, must also be rather defective; in fact, if his act of revolt is defective, then his lucidity must be defective in precisely the same degree, isn't that so? Hence in his lucidity he sees only that he has committed an error, that he is in trouble, and that he is to be made unhappy. He fires the additional shots as a gesture of disgust, disaffection, despair. Remember that in *The Myth* hope and despair are equally inadmissible, opposite sides of the same coin. The second half of the novel, which is completely necessary in every sense, thus becomes the excision or expulsion of his disgust and despair, reducing Meursault to the cold lucidity of the end of the novel. Perhaps the four shots are something related in a sense to nostalgia, or a particularly explosive instance of Sartre's nausea."

"Nausea? Call it hatred, I'd say. Nothing less. And I'm at a loss to understand why you think so well of Meursault, after all this. To my mind, he is a punk, a flyweight, beginning *and* end. Oh, I agree; the parallelism of the two parts is exact, very exact. And Meursault's hatred of the Arab and of his own complicity in the Arab's death, which is, of course, his own complicity, whether he likes it or not, in the Arab's existence, his hatred of this is precisely the same as his hatred of the mob at the end of the book; I see no advance in lucidity. An advance in his powers of analysis, if you like; but no advance toward genuine lucidity. To call his hatred a 'spirit of opposition' or 'an act of genuine revolt' is, in Meursault's case, a rationalization, I'm convinced; he is motivated throughout by hatred and rage, in which case a real lucidity is always beyond his capacity."

"He has freedom," Aspen suggested.

"Freedom? Leaving aside the fact that he is in jail for half the book, can you call it freedom when a man is so impotent that he cannot prevent himself from being led 'by chance' to the grossest imaginable crime, the murder of someone who means nothing to him? To my mind, that is the grossest imaginable determinism. And Meursault's impotence, like virtually all impotence, is a function of rage. He is blind with rage, paralyzed with rage. He is a punk, and that's the end of it."

"But chance, what you call the grossest imaginable determinism, isn't that what Camus calls simply the absurd?"

"Of course. That's my point: Meursault's crime is an element of the absurd against which he should have revolted by preventing its occurrence. That was, remember, within his power. He need not have pulled the trigger. He need not have written the letter for Raymond. Meursault was intelligent, after all, he had his fingers on the truth; but he didn't know what to do with it, and he bungled. I say he bungled to a degree that cannot be explained by absurdity or excused by fallibility. He was a punk. Only a punk would ask for jeers; in fact, that is what a punk must do."

Aspen sighed. "You make a strong case," he said.

ЛЛЛЛ

THE NEXT day Camus and Aspen went to the village in the Alfa to buy postage stamps, newspapers, stationery, tobacco, etc., etc., and afterward repaired to a café on the square. They sat at a wooden table in a small room where the owner presided at the zinc bar and the gas urn hissed drowsily. The plate windows in front were misted; only the heads of passers-by could be seen, bent against the wind and rain. A game of *trictrac* was proceeding quietly and methodically at another table, with two players and three kibitzers. Camus and Aspen flicked the pages of their newspapers. "Something to drink?" Aspen inquired. Camus answered that he would have *moka*, and when the owner came to their table, Aspen asked for two.

After a while Aspen heard a boat whistle from the direction

of the harbor, a deep, resonant, languid note. He put down his newspaper. "You know," he said, "I think that's the first time I've heard that sound in seven years, maybe eight."

"What?"

"That whistle. From the harbor."

"I didn't notice."

"A marvelous sound, really; quite beautiful."

"In itself?"

"Perhaps not, though for that matter how can you tell? But it means so much; everywhere, to everyone, isn't that so? What is it for you?"

Camus folded his newspaper. "The usual things: arrival and departure, coming and going, sadness and excitement."

"Freedom?"

"Yes, that most of all."

"And a good kind of freedom, too, isn't it? Not all hedged round with silliness. No banners, no parades, no Fourteenth of July; just something personal and rich, filled with longing and yet very real and near. On the prairies in America people used to listen this way to the train whistles, and I suppose long ago it was the postilion's bugle. Hard to imagine anyone feeling this way about the sound of a rocket engine."

"The romanticist speaking . . ."

"Yes. And not ashamed either, not the way he used to be. You know, in America romanticism was once identified with Jean-Jacques, and the worst of him at that. It has taken my generation a long time to discover that this narrow identification was not necessary."

"You mean that romance is a part of everything, and that it can be moderate and limited."

"Exactly. It's a question of human nature, and that's what we have been talking about, actually, all this time. Do you believe in it? Really and truly?"

"In human nature? Something fixed, immutable? No, I suppose not. That would be unreasonable and . . . disloyal perhaps.

But if you mean something on the order of a relative but powerful and genetically lineal endowment of propensities, if you will pardon the sesquipedalianisms, then I suppose it's undeniable, isn't it?"

"So D'Arrast was right, practically speaking, when he said that Meursault has no freedom? His nature imprisoned him?"

Camus lighted a cigarette. "No, I think D'Arrast was wrong. Because in spite of his nature, or because of it, Meursault had freed himself from many of the bonds that keep most people in chains. Of course, he could not free himself ultimately."

"And were these the things that Meursault was thinking of when he heard the boat whistle from his prison cell?"

"Undoubtedly."

"Then can you tell me now, finally, what you think of Meursault? And why D'Arrast calls him a punk?"

"D'Arrast has his reasons. As for Meursault, you must remember he was young, as I was, too, and although he understood a great deal, probably he did not understand enough."

"In what respect?"

"Oh, well. Understanding isn't a matter of this and that . . ."

"But as an example? Can you give an example?"

"There are many. But perhaps yesterday you and D'Arrast . . . you were talking about innocence, remember?"

"I remember."

"Meursault knows that men did not create history, at least not in any substantial sense, and that in consequence they cannot be guilty. But perhaps he did not understand well enough that men are the ones who keep history going. Which means, doesn't it, that they cannot be altogether innocent either? Of course, this is a moralistic way of putting it; Meursault would have deprecated it. But perhaps he was not as free from the moral categories as he wished to be. Perhaps no one is."

"Could you put it another way by saying that Meursault stood off from absurdity too far, that he placed himself too remotely in opposition to it? Whereas in reality the absurd is as much within us as without?"

"Something like that."

Aspen frowned in concentration. "Then D'Arrast's 'hatred' is too strong a term. Meursault lacks the compassion that he might have found if he had lived long enough to enlarge his understanding and apply his newly discovered lucidity; but that is not the same as hatred."

"D'Arrast would say it is a thin distinction."

"But a valid one. The point is that Meursault died, but you lived."

Camus smiled, but said nothing.

"Then is *The Stranger* less than the later books?"

"That isn't for me to say. One must abide by some of the proprieties."

"But you must have an opinion."

"I have a feeling. Which is that, in terms of form and conception, *The Stranger* is my most completely unified work, and perhaps that means it is also the most satisfying work. At any rate, everything is there, virtually everything, if only people had taken the trouble to read it carefully."

"But dozens of critics have discussed it; hundreds probably."

"Lots of criticism, yes, but not much imagination. Why do you think I have put up with this interminable interrogation of yours?"

Aspen reddened. "That's the most flattering thing anyone ever said to me, do you know that?"

Camus began to gather up his newspapers.

"One thing more," Aspen said hurriedly, "what about D'Arrast?"

"How do you mean?"

"Well . . ."

"You don't like him, do you?"

"I'm not sure. At least I don't dislike him. But something

seems wrong, or not quite explained or aboveboard, as if he had some sort of a hold over you."

"Now you're being sinister."

"Well, but is it something like that?"

"Yes, perhaps. Something."

"I see," Aspen said. "And you don't care to talk about it. Then tell me about Dora."

"What is there to tell?"

"For one thing, is she really . . . a . . . well, damn it, is she?"

"Come now, you're just being an American."

"Nevertheless, she does it for money."

"And what do you do for money . . .? Look here, do you really see any difference between Dora selling herself in her way and another woman selling herself to a factory or an office? We all sell what we have, all that we have usually, ourselves; our bodies, or some bodily attribute. Isn't that so? It's a *fact of life*. Absurd, but true. How else shall we live? Prostitution isn't an act, it's a state of mind, and as such everywhere, everywhere. I'd say Dora simply doesn't think that way."

"Have you known her long?"

"Let's say I've known her before," Camus replied. He stood up and reached for his raincoat. "Do you find her attractive?"

"Very," Aspen mumbled, rising awkwardly to his feet.

ЛЛЛЛ

[She appeared, she revealed herself. Where? Here, by God, here and last night. Opened my door and entered without so much as hello or a smile. Fantastic, a storybook thing. She was so quiet, so small, so much herself, that at last I could not help seeing what it is; she was, in her own way, frightened. What courage her life requires. She is always frightened, even more than I. "Why?" I asked; but she answered only that she is a woman and this is Europe, like a line from Camus.

You might think with two such people as we it would be no good; but it was fine. My God, I had forgotten how fine.

Afterward I was timid and hesitant, doubtful, didn't know what was expected of me. In a way, I still don't. "Why did you come?" I asked. She said that she had simply decided to; she sounded as if it were rather like deciding to walk home by one route instead of another. "Didn't you want me to come?" "Yes, yes, of course," I said, "I didn't mean anything like that." "Then why worry about it?" She was quiet for a while, and then she looked at me, seriously, and said: "I don't need any money for the present, if that's what you were thinking." She was actually concerned about my embarrassment.

For a while, a couple of hours, we were not frightened in the least. I don't suppose many people know how rapturous that cessation can be.

Her fear is different from mine; naturally, since we are different people. But without going into the clinical end at all, one can see immediately that while my feeling is always particularized and intent, hers is older, calmer, I should even say wiser; more general and, in a way, more terrible. One hesitates to use a word in ill repute, but her fear certainly gives the impression of being racial, rather than personal, in origin. Not that that makes it any the less acute.

She makes me think of the Greek women I read about as a child, the ones gifted in tragedy and endurance. Andromache, Iphigenia, Briseis. In fact, she has a metaphysical quality, not acquired, as with female poets and painters, but deeply innate; a kind of instinctual and even, one feels, organic assimilation to cosmic doubt. It is as if, fully aware of the "knowledge" of eugenics, she still carries the source of mystery in her womb.

Perhaps she is the only truly metaphysical person I have ever known.

But I still, idiot that I am, am not entirely convinced she "simply decided" to come. Why not? She gives every impression of being ingenuous. That is to say, she would never bother to tell a lie on her own account. But for someone else? She would tell dozens, without an instant's hesitation.

I am almost convinced, I am 99.99% convinced. But that infinitesimal doubt remains. Such an interweaving of doubts: is this what the return to life was bound to be? Did Camus send her? And what am I to make of D'Arrast?]

⊓⊓⊓⊓

SOME DAYS later, Camus said: "I? Naturally not. Put it down to your good luck. Or to her good sense, which comes to the same thing. But don't expect too much, for heaven's sake. As for D'Arrast, I suppose he must speak for himself."

⊓⊓⊓⊓

"NO," D'ARRAST said, "I can't accept that."

In his effort to swing the discussion toward the topic he now knew to be the most interesting, Aspen had suggested that Meursault's failure was a failure of love. Now he asked: "Well, then, what about Marie?" He turned toward Camus. "In all our talks I don't think we said two words about her."

"Perhaps there are not two words to say."

"That seems to be Meursault's opinion, at any rate, whatever you two were up to. And you have to admit Meursault's a keen observer."

"Maybe keen observers make poor lovers." Aspen subdued a giggle and his hand trembled momentarily. "Anyway, that's not the point. The point is that I think a great deal can be said about Marie. Or at least for her."

"What?"

"To begin with, the things Meursault himself says about her. She is good-looking. She is desirable. She is pleasant company. For Meursault, that's the pinnacle of ardor. I'd say she must have been rather special."

"Every woman is 'rather special,' at one time or another."

"Is that so? Well, I, for one, am grateful."

"We're all grateful," Camus said. "Marie is good for a lark, like the rest. That's what Meursault seems to be saying, and we have to take his word for it, don't we? If you're trying to lead up to what I think, then you are walking on dangerous ground."

"But why? And why do we have to take Meursault's word for it? I thought we had agreed that Meursault isn't always reliable."

"In this area I'm inclined to trust him."

"Oh."

"Another point. It seems to me you are continually trying to lead me back into regions of convention and sentimentality which I, like *all* other respectable writers of my time, have explicitly denied; and I empasize the 'all.' You want us to go backward."

"Not at all. But . . ."

"After all, what is Marie? And can you imagine Meursault married?"

"He'd make a hell of a rotten husband, that's certain. But that's exactly what I was trying to say. Don't you see, the failure is Meursault's, not Marie's."

"But you are trying to deprive him of the one undeniably

genuine element of his freedom: the freedom from conventional standards of sexual conduct; even though formerly his freedom is what you professed to admire."

D'Arrast nodded. "Yes, that's clear," he said, as if to himself.

"I still do, damn it," Aspen replied, "very much. But I don't think the question of freedom enters here. Maybe I am totally out-of-date, a prig or a sentimentalist or whatever you want to call me. But I say this: Marie has her freedom, too. An admirable freedom. She is no blue stocking; far from it, she permits herself to become Meursault's mistress on their first encounter. I'd say she is damned attractive, morally as well as sexually. Maybe she is even a bit too attractive, speaking from the point of view of verisimilitude; a bit too much the stock novelistic sex personification; without losing any of her appeal, she is still too easy a catch. But that's not the real point either. The real point is that when she asks Meursault to marry her, that has nothing to do with conventionality; she is not actuated by motives of respectability or anything like that; her previous behavior proves it. She is genuinely in love, and she is simply looking for the kind of stability in their relationship which men and women have always sought."

"Then isn't it simply that she falls in love but Meursault does not?"

"No, if you'll forgive me, that's begging the question. Doesn't Meursault make it perfectly clear, in everything he says, that he refuses on principle to fall in love, that he would never fall in love with anyone or in any circumstances?"

"You have to admit that," D'Arrast said to Camus.

With a grimace of mock asperity, Camus bowed his head.

Aspen continued: "In short, Meursault is incapable of love, whatever the reason; and like all incapacities, this one is the opposite of a freedom, it is a limitation. It has nothing whatever to do with Meursault's aspersion of bourgeois social and moral attitudes, unless you believe that, psychologically speaking, his emotional incapacity is a cause of his intellectual outlook; and I think we all would agree that this explanation is dangerously inadequate. My point is simply this: in respect to love, Marie is freer than Meursault, less limited, and she is willing to commit herself; which is, I take it, the act of a free person. Quite unconsciously, she is ready to undertake an act of revolt far more effective than Meursault's, and she invites him to join her. He refuses. Or, at any rate, he agrees for the wrong reasons, or for no reason. One can't say, I suppose, that Marie enjoys any particular lucidity, since she appears to be functioning almost entirely as a natural being, devoid of self-awareness. But in her nature she revolts instinctively, or she attempts to: she tries to engage Meursault in a quite clearly defined alliance against absurdity. She fails; or rather he does, just as he fails later, when he fires his pistol at the Arab."

"Too neat. And why do you consider marriage an act of revolt, for Pete's sake? Certainly for almost everyone, for society at large, it is just the contrary: an act of compliance, an acquiescence in social taxis. I hope you're not going to throw up at us the old rigmarole about procreation, fertility, the transmission of the living spark?"

"Hah! There you go," D'Arrast exclaimed. He turned to Aspen: "How do you say in English? He is throwing out the baby with the bathing water, eh? You may call it an old rigmarole, my friend, but a lot of people have taken it seriously, including me. Including a good many writers, too, I may say."

"Actually," Aspen interjected, "I had in mind the genuine marriage-for-love, the genuine erotic marriage. I'm inclined to agree the fertility business doesn't apply, whatever its other uses may be. We're interested in the absurdity of personal death, which isn't in the least ameliorated by the phenomenon of transpersonal propagation."

"You don't think so? I'd say it fits in precisely with your 'dignity' and your famous 'act of revolt.' If the continuance of the species in the face of death doesn't reinforce the integrity of the individual who promotes it, then I don't see—"

"Too many points of view," Camus said, interrupting. "The discussion is getting muddled." And there, for the time being, it rested.

ЛЛЛЛ

[Last night Dora said: "Do you know that you and Camus are a good deal alike? Two of a kind?"

I was astonished. "Frankly, I can't imagine two people more *un*like."

"Oh, well, in some ways, yes. But your minds work the same way."

"Bah! Our minds work the same way? Are you serious?"

"Yes."

"What are you getting at? I've always felt my mind scarcely 'worked' at all."

"Don't exaggerate," she said, frowning. She hates my nervous self-deprecations. "It's a question of attitudes, I suppose. You both have certain attitudes that you acquired long ago and you have brought them with you; you are very reluctant to change them."

"Nothing unusual in that."

"No, but the attitudes are unusual, at least for us. They're so very simple, so very black and white. You're both foreigners, you see; you're an American and Camus is an African."

"An African?"

"It must seem strange to you, I suppose. Not to us, though."

"I'd never given it quite that emphasis, at any rate. Do you think you're beginning to sound a tiny bit like the eternally superior European?"

"I don't mean to, not at all. I think most of us feel quite inferior by now."

"Meaning?"

"Everything . . ."

"Tell me what you think of Camus."

"What I'm thinking of now is his radicalism; it's so fiery and . . . so pure; or at least it once was. That's the African in him. No European radical, not even in 1870, not even in 1789, could ever manage it. We were always so aware of the complication, we were *raised* in complications . . . And all the years since he came to France, Camus has been trying to preserve that simplicity, that purity; against everything, and against himself especially. It's been pretty desperate most of the time, don't you think?"

"But perhaps that's what has kept him going. It's an idea anyway. It sets up the kind of tension he's always talking about, the state of concerned two-mindedness in which a man must write and think."

"Yes."

"Do you notice how often Camus states his case in dualities? Not the old good-and-evil, of course. For Camus a man is always hung up between two evils; instead of being attracted in two directions, he is repelled in two directions."

"For instance?"

A woman always asks for a for instance. "Well, what about the opposition between theism and humanism? That's pretty grand, it takes in virtually the whole tradition. Yet Camus rejects both, outright. Camus against the world, and the consequence is sometimes Procrustean, to say the least."

"Yes, that's what I meant, that's his radicalism."

"What about me?"

"You, you're an American."

"That goes without saying . . ."

"A sentimentalist."

"Oh?"

"Perfectly true. There isn't anything you can't turn into

sugar candy, even radicalism. Which is why I like you better . . ."

We turned to other things. But I can't say I wasn't put out
for a bit, and at first my mind wasn't on what I was doing.]

⌐⌐⌐⌐

"NO, NO, let me say something." Camus held up his hand.
"You two have been chipping away at me for a long time.
Now it's my turn."

"If we've been 'chipping away at you,' as you say," Aspen
remarked, "it's only because we wish to force you into defining your position."

"Defining my position! For the love of Mike, what have I
been doing all my life if I haven't been defining my position?"

"In your terms, yes. But we want you to use our terms."

Camus settled into his chair, and looked out the window at a
gull that was climbing the gale toward Africa. "Hmmm. I
don't say you haven't got a modicum of reason in your com-
plaint." He lighted a cigarette and propped his heels on the
windowsill, with his ankles crossed. "As a matter of fact, I
suppose that's the point of any discourse: the attempt to trans-
fer a conceptualization from one set of experiential referents
to another. All right, then, let me make a trial, at any rate.
What I was thinking is that there are a number of well-loved
women in my novels. Rieux' wife, for example, and Jan's
wife, and that girl in the Spanish play. I know, I know . . ."
He held up his hand again, forestalling interruption. "They
aren't the characters of primary importance; in fact, they are
mostly rather pathetic and ineffectual. From this, I suppose,
the reader infers that I consider love itself rather pathetic

and ineffectual, and as a matter of plain fact, if we are talking about sexual love, which seems to be the case, then the inference is not far from the truth. But it isn't the whole truth, and I should think that would have been obvious."

"Very little is obvious."

"Yes, but this is the least original part of my work, isn't it? Just an agreement with the whole modern attitude toward sex? For Pete's sake, hasn't it been discredited, time and time again? The old romantic blather? The attempt to turn women into vessels of truth, or fucking into an act of transcendence? We put that behind us long, long ago. Must we go through it all again?"

Camus flicked the ash from his cigarette into a coffee cup that rested on the tiled floor beside his chair. "It simply doesn't work, you know. Why can't we accept the ordinary data of biology? Sex is what it is, a means not an end. True, a side effect is bodily gratification; happiness, if you can call it that, such a momentary and exorbitant thing. Of all the brief forms of happiness it is the briefest, isn't it? And so nearly unconscious that it can scarcely be considered a happiness at all."

"But . . ." Aspen was cut short.

"No, I insist, let me finish. In any case, I anticipate what you are going to say: that I am taking sex in its crudest sense, that many refinements are possible and, given human sensibility, natural, that the happiness of sexual love extends into other spheres of behavior, etc., etc. Isn't that it? All right, I grant your point; and I still say that sex is ineluctably transitory and burdened with pain, guilt, frustration, selfishness, and crime. Isn't that the whole experience of our time? Isn't the evidence spread out in nauseating abundance in our press, our art, our police courts, in the look of our faces among the crowd, in the constriction of our own tortured hearts? Is there one of us who hasn't known the loss, betrayal, crassitude, filth, moronism, and above all the attrition and fatigue, of love? I ask you. Tell me it isn't so, if you can." Camus looked directly at Aspen.

"Often enough . . ."

"Very well. That was what Marie offered Meursault; precisely that. And he had the good sense to turn it down. Not that he wouldn't have married her if she wanted it, he said he would, but he suffered no delusion about what he was doing; none whatever. He knew that Marie could not help him in the least. In that respect, Meursault was, I must say, as clear-headed as anyone could ask."

Camus dropped the stub of his cigarette into the coffee cup, where it hissed briefly. "But love . . ." He frowned slightly. "Love, real love, is something else again. You are quite correct, I think, in saying that Meursault's error, the flaw in his personality which prevented him from acquiring genuine lucidity at the point when it could have helped him in a practical way, lay in the region of feeling. Not much to do with Marie, I'd say, but a great deal to do with . . . call it what you will; compassion, magnanimity; sometimes I have called it solidarity."

"Christian love?"

"In the sense that it was the kind of love recommended by Jesus of Nazareth, yes. But you have to dissociate it from centuries of theology and the church, which is often difficult to do. I prefer to use the term only on special occasions." Camus scratched his head. "The point is this: something transitory, painful, and grounded solely in physiology, in short, sexual love, can never constitute a revolt; can never constitute, for that matter, a metaphysical act of any description. But what we call solidarity, on the other hand, if it is expressly and consciously applied, can certainly take form as an attitude of genuine revolt, issuing in acts of genuine revolt; and the reason is precisely because it is grounded, not in physiological necessity, but in ethical necessity, as I have taken considerable pains to point out in *The Rebel* and elsewhere."

D'Arrast said: "You are sounding, if I may say so, rather like an academician."

"Yes," Camus said, laughing. "You are right. Well, one gets wound up, it's a fault of mine. But do you agree with me, generally speaking?"

"Very profoundly."

"And you?"

"Yes, of course," Aspen said. "As profoundly as D'Arrast, I imagine. But I have a little disagreement, too. You tell us of the modern disenchantment with romantic, no, erotic love, and of course you are right; one doesn't dare dispute the sociologists. But isn't it still possible that in the right circumstances erotic love can overcome the pain and frustration, can grow into something more or less enduring, can provide a truly self-conscious happiness, and can even expand into the general attitude of solidarity which you describe? I believe it; I believe it just as profoundly as I believe that solidarity is essential to rebellion and the general welfare. I have seen it. And you must have, too; otherwise you could not have written about Dr. Rieux and his wife in the way you did."

"I don't say it can never happen. I only say that when it does happen it is fortuitous. There is no necessity in it, not even an esthetic necessity; which would be only justice, if there were such a thing as justice. Sex is grounded in physiology; in other words, in mere bodily circumstance; and the only necessity engendered by bodily circumstance is the mechanical bodily response."

"Circumstance? Response? I don't follow. We are all physiological beings before we are anything else; that is our endowment, our being, if we have any. What could be less fortuitous? No, it seems to me that a necessity grounded in our physical natures is the most firmly grounded of any. The pain, the frustrations, the transitoriness, these are the fortuities, introduced into our erotic existences by the absurdities of death and society. But erotic love itself is genuine, and when it is consciously and intelligently elaborated, in the creativeness of the dynamic sensibility, it becomes a genuine act of revolt, a genuine self-assertion, leading to lucidity, happiness, and dignity."

"You might almost have persuaded me if you hadn't added 'dignity.' The two-backed beast? Come, that is pure compulsion, nothing more."

Aspen spoke slowly: "On this point we cannot agree, then. A compulsion, yes; more than that, an imperfection, in itself imperfect and a sign of eternal human imperfectibility and incompleteness. Who would not be pure spirit if he could choose? But I thought that was just what we were saying, that absurdity is everywhere, in everything, every act and feeling and thought, and that we have no choice. We work with what we have, isn't that right? With what we understand? We choose to be what we are, and then to make the most of it, in spite of and in the midst of absurdity. And in that very making, that choosing and striving, love reaches a lucidity greater than that which derives from the simple confrontation of the individual consciousness with death. It turns the experience of its own eternal imperfectibility into an enrichment, a cause for further and further measures of love. And the result is happiness, the result is rejoicing, in the body and in the heart; and the result is revolt, too, a real revolt, a *joined* revolt, not simply a stranger crying in the wilderness. That is what I believe, at any rate."

"It's a point," Camus said.

ᒥᒪᒥᒪ

OF THE group, Dora spoke the least, and her words were brief and pointed: "Love came first, you know. It works logically. You can't have a negative without a prior positive, nor a part without a prior whole. Love is the ground from which all other feelings rise by differentiation, a differentiation so radical in some cases that we are accustomed to call its products, such as envy and jealousy, the opposites of love; but this is merely a convenience, for they cannot exist without love. Women know the truth. Aside from logic, do you suppose the foetus in the womb feels anything but love? A crude love, doubtless; but love, complete and unquestioned. Any other affection, in those circumstances, is inconceivable, a non-thing. Love is the only knowledge the foetus has of its environment. Later this love burgeons into the entire affective equipment of the individual being, his personality, whatever it may be."

No one spoke for a moment. Then Camus: "What you are saying is that hatred begins with parturition."

"Of course. That was Meursault's error. He took his birth too seriously."

⌐⌐⌐⌐

[The way she and the Alfa suit each other, it's . . . it's like everything else about her, miraculous. In my circumstances the term has real meaning. I couldn't be more pleased and astonished if Nefertiti herself stepped into my room at this moment and said how-do-you-do. Dora takes to the Alfa as warmly as I. It's like the perfect last stroke of a painting, they are both so trim and true. When I step out to get something in a shop, and then return and find her face behind the glass, a small brown smile for me, every time I am overcome again. Those two marks between her eyebrows, frown-marks, marks of concentrated spirit, how lovely they are. And I've never got them on paper correctly. Probably never will. A mistake to try. Actually, there are hundreds of things to say about her, hundreds, but no time. We are busy, busy; here, there, everywhere; but until now never far from this house. I wonder when that will be. Soon, perhaps. The main thing: happiness is possible.]

ЛЛЛЛ

IN DECEMBER the rain ceased, the wind changed quarter, the sun shone: the days were almost warm. All at once Aspen saw the mythic foundation beneath the culture of the Mediterranean. Upon the hills and cliffs, above the sea, he could visualize pageants and processions winding, banners, tambourins, and bells. In some parts of the world, Judea, although still remote and strange, is nevertheless conceivable.

Early one morning, Aspen and D'Arrast, who were up before the others, found themselves in the kitchen together. Their relationship was straightforward but laconic, and touched with a certain distance. Aspen, in the recklessness of his new-found exuberance, decided to bring the matter to a point of determination. He was sitting at a white enameled table, on which rested a bowl of oranges, a plate of rolls, and two empty cups. He said to D'Arrast, who was standing before a small gas stove: "Is it Dora?"

D'Arrast turned, bringing a conical glass coffee-pot to the table. He poured a cup of coffee for each of them, then sat down and began to wrench the skin from an orange. "Not exactly," he said.

"Not exactly? I don't understand."

"If she hasn't told you, then how could you?" D'Arrast pushed a section of orange into his mouth, made a hollow fist, and spat the seeds into it. "Look here, it's nothing to do with you, you can be assured of that. Jealous, yes; who wouldn't be, of such a woman? But I can't do anything about it, nothing whatever. She is free and she has chosen." He shrugged. "Congratulations, I suppose. In my position, what else . . ." He broke off. Then: "She really hasn't told you about it?"

"No."

"I should have known. And in that case I won't either. Let's simply say that in my position I cannot make any claims for myself. None whatever. You need feel no compunction, and I may say I think you're lucky, damn lucky, though some people wouldn't agree . . . I hope you'll treat her decently." He finished his orange and pushed the peelings to one side. "However, that's none of my business. I probably won't be here much longer anyway."

"I see. Or rather I don't. It does have something to do with Camus, doesn't it? I mean your 'position'?"

"In a way."

"Is that why he's been so . . . so touchy these past few weeks?"

"Partly. But you haven't helped matters either, you know. You've been jabbing him in a particularly sensitive area."

"What do you mean?"

"Call it romance. Lots of artists have to fight against their own instincts, I gather; that's where they get their strength, their discipline. Okay, romance is his instinct, a very deep one, I'd say, and as an artist he has to exclude it. He knows if he permitted himself to follow his bent, he'd be overboard in a minute, and he's deathly afraid of it."

"Why afraid?"

"Hard to say. The public aspect is clear enough, I suppose. He believes he has something important to do; he is driven, year in and year out, by his responsibility to his own reason, which becomes, by extension and identity, his responsibility to reason in general, and to the world. But he thinks that if he permits his work to rest in the phase of development which is easy and natural, if he permits it to remain merely art in the old sense, storytelling, romancing, entertaining, then his responsibility will be muddled and he won't be taken seriously."

"Many artists would consider that a mistake. Even a disloyalty."

"Maybe it is, I don't know. I'm not an artist."

"You think there is more to his fear than this? Something private?"

D'Arrast filled their cups again. "I suspect it. But that's as far as it goes. Sometimes he has behaved as if he were afraid of romance in himself, in his own heart and mind; afraid of some catastrophe that romance entails. In a way, all of us have the same fear, of course, but with him it's exaggerated, I don't know why. Perhaps long ago something happened . . ."

D'Arrast broke off. Camus himself, wearing a maroon bathrobe and smoking a cigarette, stood in the doorway.

_∏_∏_∏_∏

"YOU KNOW," D'Arrast said, "in a way Dora is right. I got out the novel again last night, I was reading it, and suddenly for the first time I realized who is the really important person, the one the book is about. Do you know who?"

Camus asked, smiling: "Who?"

"The mother. It's perfectly clear, she is the one who opens the book and closes it: Meursault begins by saying she has died and ends by realizing her happiness. The whole novel is about her. But more than that, the whole novel is *inside* her; embodied by her, enclosed by her; figuratively speaking, of course. And that's as it should be. It's a novel of birth, isn't it? That's what Dora said. Meursault's birth, or rebirth; his renaissance. Naturally, Meursault lives inside his mother, in the womb. Where else can he live?" D'Arrast raised his finger, excitedly. "And who is she, the mother? Not named, not once in the whole novel, scarcely even described, although her presence is felt, I see now, in every word. Every word. Of course she *cannot* be named; she is *the* mother, *our* mother, Earth, Rhea, Cybele, Mother Nature. My God, what an idea. It works in a hundred ways at once. Do you know Rhea's children? I looked them up: Zeus, Hades, Poseidon, Hera, Hestia, Demeter; all the attributes of existence; life and death; Meursault!"

"And what does Meursault mean?" Aspen asked, caught up in D'Arrast's enthusiasm. "Literally, that is?"

"It's the name of a village," Dora said.

"Where they make an excellent white burgundy," D'Arrast continued. "And wine is by no means beside the point. But listen to this: Meursault; meurs, sot; die, you idiot! Perfect, isn't it? And he could just as well have been called Naissault. What do you say to that?"

"There was another novel at one point," Camus remarked, somewhat lazily. "About a fellow called Mersault. I only added a letter."

"Mersault! Then the sea is in it, too, the salt sea, the lonely sea, the single or singular sea. Salt of death, savor of death. Death of salvation. All these things, the fruits of the earth. And yet the earth, the mother, is the enduring factor, the beginning and the end. How does it go, that rhetoric: 'As it was in the beginning, so it is and ever shall be'? Ah, the meanings, the meanings! I tell you, Camus, whether you like it or not you have written a novel of generation."

"Secrets of the shop, secrets of the guild," Camus intoned, as if he were repeating an oath, "shall not be divulged to the uninitiated."

"Bah."

"Of course, of course." Aspen took up the thread, excitedly. "And you can go further. Meursault is all these things and

more. Don't you sometimes have the feeling that the whole
novel is a dream, that it is all occurring inside Meursault's
head, all the characters are only different personifications of
his own being, Raymond, the magistrate, the robot woman,
even Salamano's dog? Yes, it's true; it's a perfect surrealism;
perfect because it is so real; perfect because it emerges by
imperceptible degrees from the concrete data of experience.
What could be better, more true, more representative of the
hallucination of life? Do you remember the trial, the scene
in the courtroom, when Meursault imagines that he is one of
the spectators looking at himself? But of course, that is precisely what he is. He is everyone in the book, everyone in
the world. You, me, Camus himself. What a vision! It's like
one of those old paintings of the last judgment, so crowded
with faces that no matter how often you look you always
see someone new, yet all there on the canvas, held within
the frame. No wonder we can spend so much time talking
about it, it is the myth of all mankind, the myth of the un-
fathomable person."

"You know what I think," Camus said. "I think you're a
couple of fantasts."

"So do I," Dora said.

⊓⊔⊓⊔⊓

[Of course I've asked Dora, more than once, who the hell this
D'Arrast is; but she always, frowning, replies that I'll find out
someday, and if I don't, what difference does it make? As far
as that goes, I guess she's right.]

⊓⊔⊓⊔⊓

"SPEAKING OF names," D'Arrast said to Aspen, one afternoon when they met briefly under the loggia in back, "do you know what Dora means?"

"No."

"It means gift."

"I see."

Clear enough. And later, when Aspen looked it up to make sure, he found the idea extending in several directions. *Dora* is cognate, for instance, to *dowry*, "a woman's marriage portion, the income of which belongs to the husband during coverture."

"Indeed," Aspen muttered, closing the dictionary softly.

⊓⊔⊓⊔⊓

AS THEY came nearer to Christmas, Dora and Aspen found themselves, unexpectedly, imbued with intimations of enlarging sensibilities; a feeling manifestly not shared by Camus and D'Arrast. It was as if the atmosphere itself had become, for the lovers, heady and aromatic, at first unnoticeably but then more plainly. Indeed, the weather remained fine; the days were warm and bright, and after dark the sky was brilliant with stars, reaching across the sea toward Africa like a huge Arabian carpet. One night Aspen began sketching camels on his sketch pad, and at first was unable to imagine why, until he remembered these were the beasts of the Three

Kings, favorite motifs for Christmas cards. Then he drew camels dancing and sleeping and copulating and feasting; among the palm trees, under the stars.

Dora said that she wished to give Aspen a Christmas present, adding: "You have afflicted me, now I am a sentimentalist, too." But she hadn't enough money. When Aspen removed his billfold from his pocket, she said: "No, that would be as if you were buying your own present, you would know exactly how much it is. It spoils the surprise. Why don't I sell something?" Aspen pressed his forefinger against her brow, leaving a faint red impression. "But my dear Sahibah," he intoned, with a mock-Hindu accent, "you have nothing, now, to sell." He ended by giving her a blank check.

On the third Sunday of Advent, Dora attended church, alone and in the evening. Camus, D'Arrast, and Aspen sat with their coffee in the room with the blue and white floor; Camus and D'Arrast sweetened their coffee with anisette, which Aspen declined. Beyond the balcony, the polished limbs of the dead trees gleamed faintly in starlight, and the sea, below, moved obscurely, like a moth-eaten tapestry. "What do you suppose Dora gets out of going to church?" Camus asked. "Is she religious?"

"I don't think so," Aspen said.

"Certainly not in the ordinary sense," D'Arrast explained, with a glance, possibly signifying apology, at Aspen. "There is no commitment to dogma, at any rate; quite the contrary. But the church means more than that, something quite different, I think, to Dora and probably to ninety per cent of the other people who are occasional church-goers. It means fellowship of a very profound sort, doesn't it? Being together, communion? It means belonging to the human race, and what else is there that has the same . . . the same catholicity? I suppose at times the need to express these sentiments is rather strong," he concluded drily.

Camus sighed. "Of course, of course. Still, one has one's

convictions. No matter how deeply one longs for communion, one does not commit oneself to ceremonies in praise of ideas which one holds to be irretrievably incomprehensible. The dogma is there, you know."

"Not obtrusively, though. Especially at times like this. It's the nonbelievers like you who are always so damned conscious of the dogmatic side of it. Most people feel that being *that* conscientious in itself destroys the communion, quite aside from the ideas as such; though possibly this is more a woman's point of view than a man's. Nevertheless, you must admit the church is remarkably easygoing on the whole, and has been for ages. You may go to service with cotton stuffed in your ears, you may cross your fingers during the *credo*, you may conjugate Latin verbs while the priest delivers his sermon. No one will object as long as you don't make a disturbance."

"Yes, and you haven't been to church in thirty years, you old reprobate. Why don't you go soak your head?" Camus turned to Aspen. "You see what he's leading up to, don't you?"

"As a matter of fact, I don't think I do."

"You don't know? Dora hasn't told you?"

"Told me what?"

"There's loyalty for you, D'Arrast. Why don't you recruit her for your . . . your organization? Though for that matter, I hope you don't." Then to Aspen: "D'Arrast is from Algeria."

"Ah . . ."

"From the F.L.N."

Aspen blinked. "Of course, of bloody course, what a jughead I am! Tell me, how could I have failed to guess?" He smiled ruefully. "I may say, D'Arrast, at the risk of sounding jejune, I'm suddenly absolutely delighted to make your acquaintance."

"Well, you know, I thought you might be; you have the right kind of indignation. A word of caution, however; or rather, two words. First, you will keep quiet about this, of course, but remember that even an inadvertent disclosure to the wrong person, even a word or a look that doesn't mean anything to you, might cost me my life. And a lot of other people their lives, too. Second, bear in mind it isn't altogether wise to know me, especially here and now, in this country. It's risky; things do happen. So be careful."

"Naturally. Don't worry about me. You're here, I suppose because you want to . . ."

"Because he wants," Camus said, interrupting, "to persuade me to make a public statement totally disavowing the French cause in Algeria." He got up and went to the window. "Me, a Frenchman!" He rapped on the glass with his fingernail.

"Why not?" D'Arrast asked. "I'm a Frenchman."

Camus turned around. "Yes, and you're also a professional . . . a professional what-you-may-call-'em."

"A mercenary?"

"No, I don't mean that, of course." Camus returned to his chair, and spoke more calmly. "But at least you are professionally committed, and without words, mind you, without words. That's the important thing. I am the one who must speak, write, make distinctions, play advocate to the public conscience; not you." He rubbed his chin with the back of his hand, rasping his whiskers. "Anyway, what earthly good could it do?"

"We think a statement from a man in your position . . ."

"My position, my position! I wish to heaven I had no position."

D'Arrast spoke to Aspen: "You see how closely we have been striking at this issue in our recent conversations. The question of compassion, of love . . . And the question of justice."

"Love and justice, precisely," Camus said. "That is the point I have spent the entire last decade trying to make clear. They are incompatible, no? Not always, of course; but a good deal of the time; and when they conflict, a tension is set into being which can be helpful, not hurtful, to the individual person. Maybe we shouldn't be so quick to remove all the tensions from the world. Mind you, I'm not attempting to establish a universal psychology, I'm merely saying that it works for me: I have found that my existence in this state of tension, in spite of its discomforts, spurs me to thought, to creative action, to . . . art."

"No doubt. And I'm sure many people share your experience. But now it is not a question of art, old friend. And it is not a question of a simple conflict. Justice and compassion are mixed now, not opposed, which I take to be just the condition most likely to reduce the individual person to paralysis. At least, that seems to be the case with you."

"Not at all. I have declared my position with a good deal of pertinacity, if I say so myself."

"You have said, in effect, that you refuse to act. But action is required now, not art, not writing. Your declarations seem to me nothing but a willed ratification of a prior incapacity, brought about by your paralysis."

"You are being terribly hard on me, D'Arrast. Do you realize how hard?" Camus turned to Aspen. "In spite of what he says, you know, D'Arrast doesn't admit there can be any justice except on the Arab side." He leaned back in his chair. "Well, there is much justice, much justice, attending the Arabs, as I have said often, time and again; and with what feeling you, who are my friends, ought to know. Deprivation, oppression, poverty, all the rest: do you think I have not seen it in my lifetime, seen it, reported it, despised it? The point needs no argument. But there is a French justice, too, an Algerian French justice, and to deny it is just as evil as to deny the Arabs their dignity and freedom. What do they ask for, the Arabs? Dignity and freedom, yes, but also separation, national separation, and beyond that, dominance and revenge. This is something else again, something wild, emotional, irrational. Dignity and freedom are qualities they will find within France, not without it. There has never been an Algerian nation, not in all history. Nor do the Arabs make up all of Algeria; the Jews, Turks, Greeks, Italians, Berbers, what of them? And the size and seniority of the French community cannot be denied. As for the Arabs, their dream of independence is fantastic, because they have no nationhood. They have only Islam, an historical empire based on religion, which Nasser is attempting to revive. That's the key, isn't it? Not nationalism, but imperialism, a new empire. And we know what to think of imperial justice."

Camus paused, no one said anything, and he went on. "I've said it all before, hundreds of times. And I've said what I think must be done, too, for anyone who cared to listen. A truce, of course; a truce first of all, a stop to the terrorization of civilians: what a way to conduct a political discussion! Why should innocent French women be required to risk a grenade every time they go out to shop for dinner? Why should innocent French children be bombed in their schoolrooms? For that matter, why should innocent Arabs be cut down in the street simply because they have French friends? A senseless, hideous business. Remember," he said in a brisker tone, turning toward Aspen, "the Algerian French are natives, too. Algeria is their country, the only country they have known in all their lives; most of them, anyway. Well, after the truce, what? The government has muddled, of course; that goes without saying; extemporized and equivocated, as usual. There should have been a clear policy from the beginning: absolute end to colonialism, on one hand, and restoration of freedom and dignity to the Arab people; but, on the other, no forfeiture whatever of the rights of the Algerian French." He paused again, and went on. "I know. That is where the difficulty begins. But a *practical* difficulty, do you see? Not ideological. And I refuse to believe a solution cannot be worked out on practical grounds, if the will to do so exists. Integration of Algeria into metropolitan France, representation in the national

parliament on a strict proportional basis, something like that."
He shrugged almost imperceptibly. "But let the killing stop,
let the terror come to an end. Above all, don't ask me to
contribute to it." He nodded toward the window. "At this
moment some poor bastard over there, under those bright
stars, is learning what it's like to have a serving of steel in his
belly, instead of bouillabaisse. Perhaps a friend of mine. If you
weren't here," he said to D'Arrast, "I'd be thinking it might
be you."

Camus said no more, and the silence thickened around them.

Finally Aspen spoke. "Perhaps an outsider shouldn't horn
in, perhaps you will simply disdain whatever I say, yet when
an issue arises which engages the conscience of the species,
everyone is obliged to speak his thoughts. And Camus, good
friend, I am saddened to hear you speak yours, because they
seem a betrayal of your own deepest convictions, they seem
a consequence of blindness, not lucidity. Dignity and freedom,
these are your terms, and we have spoken also of integrity,
the self in revolt, happiness, and so on. Do not these things
override other considerations? Are not these precisely what
the Arabs are seeking? Is this not a genuine rebellion? Then
how can you talk of suppressing it?" Camus stirred, but Aspen
went on. "I know, in my country we once suppressed a rebellion. But at least we were a real nation, culturally and histori-
cally, and even if the North had in some respects made an
economic dependency of the South, there was never any
question of colonialism, not at all; and this is aside from the
question of slavery, which was, in spite of scholarly equivocation among historians, the fundamental issue in the minds of
most of those who were engaged in the contest. It still is the
fundamental issue. I am an abolitionist to this moment; and
you also, if I have read you rightly: there can be no temporiz-
ing. Your argument that the Arabs are not a nation . . . I
hope you won't be offended if I say it sounds so naïve that
it is completely out of character. Every nation must begin

sometime, I suppose; let the Arabs begin now if they wish. As you once said to me in another connection, things like nationhood are less outward forms than states of mind, and I'd say the Arabs are thinking, the best of them, in quite genuinely, legitimately nationalistic terms. And can the Algerian French really be natives when they have never assimilated themselves to the culture of the land in which they are living, when they are the remnants of a clearly occupying power and an oligarchical regime? I'd say this is a poor definition of the term, certainly an unusual one. Have the French won more seniority in one hundred years than the Arabs in five hundred? And what are the 'rights' of the Algerian French? Certainly no more than the rights of any minority; that is to say, the rights of personal liberty and privacy. These have nothing to do with the privileges which have been arrogated during a century of colonialism and against which the Arabs are in revolt. Yet your statement appears to defend not only the rights but the privileges as well, as if the privileges could be justified simply by appeal to their own existence or because most of the Algerian French were born in Algeria instead of in France."

"No, no, that is going too far, that is more than you can say legitimately." D'Arrast was speaking, but almost as if in the voice of Camus. "No doubt that is the way it may appear to you as an outsider, which is your own term. But you, too, are oversimplifying the reality. The truth is that I really do not believe all justice is on the side of the Arabs. All justice? We are agreed, aren't we, that absolute justice is a fiction, a dream, perhaps the noblest and most beautiful ever conceived, but still an impossibility. All we can say is that each individual being is born with a claim to justice, an equal claim but a claim which can never be satisfied. And beyond that . . . well, the claims grow muddled as they act on one another, combining and conflicting, and they become, ultimately, like all things, matters of interpretation. God help us, if there were a god. In the present case, the claims of the Algerian French are not only those which you call the claims of the minority, but perhaps also claims of history, claims of the land, claims of the heart; these, too, are important, beyond the legalistic considerations. And all these claims are howling for justice, pitiably and in a sense foolishly; because justice, true justice, is a fiction. For my part, I believe with my whole mind that an immense *preponderance* of justice resides in the Arab cause, and I believe this so deeply that I actually cannot imagine anyone truly believing otherwise: the other side, the army, the bureaucracy, etc., seems to me composed merely of scoundrels. And yet I cannot escape, logically, from the experience of my time: justice is relative, which is another way of saying that it is a fiction. This detracts nothing whatever from my justice, but by the same token it leaves the other fellow's also intact, however small it may be; and the issue between us is arguable. That is why," he said, turning to Camus, "I have lately shifted the ground of my appeal from the claim of justice to the claim of compassion. Can you deny the appeal of those millions who are suffering, exactly those for whom your writing and your life have cried out in the past?"

"Can I deny the appeal of my mother?" Camus said simply. Then to Aspen: "Yes, she is there, in Algiers." He nodded again toward the window. "At this moment, for all I know, it is she who is eating the supper of steel."

"You have a terrible choice, Camus." D'Arrast's voice was guttural. "But can you evade it, millions against one?"

"My friend, we are talking about life now, aren't we, life and death? We have passed beyond the relative; and beyond the absolute, too, if there is such a thing. A life, as long as it lasts, is indivisible and equivalent. Your millions against one is a false proportion, and your choice is not a choice at all."

"You cannot choose?"

"I have one loyalty before all others: to my own decision

that I will not murder or connive in murder. That is my plenary rebellion, that is the indispensable assertion of myself against absurdity. If you tell me that I may save Monsieur A only at the expense of Monsieur B, or vice versa, I have no choice. That is to say, in those circumstances the act of choosing falls outside any rational category; it is inconceivable. And it makes no difference if one side is numerically weighted against the other. Life, I repeat, is equivalent."

"You cannot choose?"

"I cannot."

"Then you cannot act."

"Not in that sense."

"In what sense then?"

"I can think. I can suffer. I can write."

"Then your rebellion is not an act, but a fiction. Its meaning is not ethical, but esthetic. And for you the very meaning of your existence passes from the actual to the imagined, and you are no better than the conventional *homme d'esprit*."

"Oh, D'Arrast. Do you think I have not foreseen this? Months ago, years ago? Do you think I have not driven myself like a rat into this same corner, again and again? Let be, if you can, let be. I must find my strength."

part five

⌐⌐⌐⌐

THE GROUP dispersed a few days before Christmas, agreeing to meet again afterward. Dora and Aspen loaded suitcases, paints, books, the stone, and blankets into the Alfa's small luggage compartment, and drove off eastward: the movement toward independence, the assertion of themselves apart, toward which they had known the momentum of their lives was carrying them. Through the bright day, the Alfa sped, humming on the straights, growling on the turns, as Aspen, low in his seat, savored his affiliation with the car, the road, the land, and the universe. In the Piedmont, above Turino, they found a stone cottage which overlooked a village, nearly hidden among thick groves of spruce, with scraggly juniper growing beside the paths. The weather changed; snow fell on Christmas Eve. Dora and Aspen mingled with the villagers in the feathery air: at wineshop, square, and church, with torchlight and singing. The next day was bright and clear, and the sunlight gleamed on the snow-laden spruces. Dora and Aspen stayed in bed all day.

Dora's gift to Aspen was a small ship's compass from the late eighteenth century, teak inlaid with rosettes of amber. Later Aspen fixed it, by means of a spring clip, to the gearbox housing of the Alfa, ahead of the shift stick.

On Christmas Day they spoke of Camus. "What do you think?" Aspen asked. "Was D'Arrast right when he called him a conventional *homme d'esprit*?"

Dora answered, "No," and said that for her Camus had always been simply a man; which was everything.

"Yes, and the novels prove it, don't they?"

"And the stories and essays and plays. Everything."

"The quality of sympathy is unmistakable; that's certain. Nothing academic about it, nothing learned or imitated; it's part of his innate equipment. Which is what saves it from ever being corny or maudlin, I suppose. In essence, he is humane, and so his books are, too; which is everything, as you say. But if that's the case, why is he so muddled over the Algerian business?"

"His mother does live there. His brother, too, I think."

"You mean he's too close to it, too deeply involved? A case of the successful statesman who can't solve a crisis in his own household?"

"Something like that."

"Yes, and it's a good reason, too, though a lot of idiots wouldn't think so. The humane person, the relativist, doesn't expect, in one lifetime, to find clarity of thought in more than one or two compartments of his mind, though that doesn't excuse him from pressing his search among the rest of the ruins. Yet judging from his manner and expression, there's something more than this at the root of the present crisis."

"He's writing a book."

"What?"

"He's writing a book."

"I'll be damned. It's plain as a pikestaff, though, when you stop to consider. He has all the symptoms. But why didn't I guess?"

"Women have a knack for such things. Besides, he told me."

"He told you?"

"After I asked."

"I'll be damned. What is it?"

"A novel. But he wouldn't say what about."

"You think it's connected with what we were talking about? Back there?" Aspen fluttered his hand in the direction of France.

"Oh, yes. That's certain, I should think."

"Why?"

"Camus doesn't mark time, you notice; not often. In one sense, everything with him is repetition and restatement, but in another sense, everything is an advance, too, even the little essays and editorials. As likely as not, they are little steps leading to the next big leap."

"A big leap is in order, all right."

"He said it himself."

"You mean when he said he had worked himself into a corner?"

"Yes. And he's his own best critic, remember. That's why the spectacle of you and D'Arrast chipping away at him, as he said, is a little ridiculous in a way."

"I'm sure. Nevertheless, D'Arrast and I arrived at the same point as Camus, the same corner. How do you explain that?"

"Similarities of experience and concern, broadly speaking. But neither of you is driven by the same necessity that drives Camus."

"I'm not so sure of that." Aspen got up and went to the window, where he looked out into the snow-covered forest, squinting against the snow-reflected brilliance. "Anyway, that's not the point," he said finally, turning around. "Tell me, how do you define the corner?"

Dora was in bed, sitting against the headboard with her knees drawn up beneath the counterpane. "I'm sure he has his own terms worked out," she said, "and undoubtedly they'll surprise us when we hear them. But I should think it must reduce itself to a question of the man we were talking about at first, the humane person."

"A conflict of sense and sensibility?"

"At bottom, though undoubtedly there is some of each on both sides." She locked her fingers behind her head, and gazed into the stone fireplace at the side of the room. "He has to have his revolt, you see? That's basic, that's the *sine qua non*. Revolt is the only means for confronting the absurdity of life. Except suicide, of course, which he instinctively reviles. But revolt entails its own contradiction: in order to revolt, in order to assert one's own claim for life and individuality, one must acknowledge the same claim for everyone else. This is where compassion comes in; and this is also, incidentally, where Meursault's concept of revolt is shown to be extremely immature. Camus was immature at one time himself, like all of us, but the point is that he changed, he made the acknowledgment. And then he had to write a whole book, *The Rebel*, in which he redefined his concept of revolt, modified, explained, rewrote it, until he wound up with the idea, in effect, that the only ethical revolt, the only revolt which accepts the claims of others, the only philosophically safe revolt, in other words, is that of the artist. At first he was satisfied with this, I think, but then he came to recognize, as D'Arrast pointed out, that there wasn't much difference between his view and that of the conventional *homme d'esprit*."

"The old business about art creating reality, style creating meaning, expressionism, all that?"

"Yes. And if there's one thing Camus can't stomach, that's it. If only because he was in the thick of the Resistance. He knows there is no style in a Gauleiter's execution order; but there's a lot of meaning, a lot of reality."

"Very good." Aspen went to the fireplace and pushed one of the logs with the toe of his slipper, sending a shower of sparks up the chimney. "His compassion, which was an outcome of his revolt, has forced him to adopt the concept of the safe revolt, as you call it so aptly. Yet the concept of a safe revolt is deeply contrary to the whole tone and feeling of the man."

"Exactly."

"But what about his theory of limits?"

"It's a good theory, workable and reasonable. The trouble is he's afraid he has gone too far. A revolt that limits itself is one thing, a revolt that puts itself out of action is another. And he's afraid that his retreat into art has really been a retreat into inaction. He is a realist, as much as you, remember; he doesn't have any illusions about the practical efficacy of art. And I don't think he has much illusion about his precious trade-union movement either, I mean in the realm of practical efficacy. What he says about it in *The Rebel*, aside from being perfunctory, has a sort of hollow ring about it, like whistling in the dark. It's a cut-and-dried matter now, trade unionism, the predictable assertion of predictable economic rights. Not much creativeness there, and hence not much real revolt."

"The real, or unsafe, revolt that is nevertheless compassionate: is that a fair statement of the corner?"

"It's one. I suppose there are others."

"It's a damn good one, at any rate. And you're a marvel."

"Nonsense. I've just been listening for the past six weeks, while the rest of you have been talking."

Aspen bowed gravely from the waist, like a Chinese prime minister, and climbed back into bed.

_Π_Π_Π_Π

THE NEXT morning, Aspen, in a reckless fit, borrowed a pair of skis from a group of young people who passed the cottage, and set off down the path to the village. As long as his progress was unimpeded, he attained a somewhat higher rate of acceleration than he had expected, but at the end of fifty yards the toe of his left ski snagged in a juniper, and he went down, vertiginously. The pain in his leg seemed, for some moments, impossible; an evil miracle. Then he threw up and then he fainted. In the hospital at Turino, he was told that the ankle joint was critically wrenched, and the talus cracked.

With his leg, caked in plaster to the knee, resting on an

improvised hassock, Aspen spent the night dozing in an armchair before the fire. Dora slept in the bed. About once an
hour she woke up and asked if he wanted anything, to which
he responded, "No." Even so, she got up several times, tended
the fire, brewed tea, adjusted his pillows, helped him to the
toilet; she offered to help him into bed. Aspen refused. "You'd
be more comfortable," she pointed out, reasonably. Aspen
muttered that sometimes a man had to give himself up to his
own assininity. Nevertheless, toward morning he slept soundly
in his chair for several hours, and awoke with a raging hunger
when he smelled coffee and frying meat.

They set off after breakfast. With his leg hoisted on pillows which Dora had strewn on the floor of the cockpit, Aspen
said he felt fine. The day was bright, cold, and pretty; the
highway was dry, although patched here and there with snow.
Dora drove skillfully and carefully. At the frontier, the customs
officer looked at Aspen's American passport and asked him if
he wished to declare his broken leg. Aspen grinned comically,
at the same time wishing he had given the idiot a frozen stare.

By noontime, Aspen's leg was throbbing painfully and he
was feverish. They stopped to rest at an inn, took broth and
an omelet for their lunch, but decided, after a mincing discussion, to stay the night. Their room was rather grand, as it
turned out, with darkly polished wood, cut in shapes of lancet
and pilaster, and a well-made fire. "I suppose this might do for
a castle," Aspen mumbled, as he hunkered into the armchair,
"as well as any place else."

"That's what you want, a castle?"

"More or less."

"I'd be afraid to give you one, supposing I could." Dora was
moving about the room, hanging garments in the wardrobe
and laying out articles on the dressing table. "You'd probably
go hide again at the top of the tower."

"Not much danger of that."

"Can you be so sure?"

Aspen grunted. "For that matter, I suppose I'll always be living in my hidden room, one way or another. But I don't think the actual forms of one's misery are likely to repeat themselves."

"Many people would disagree." She stood with one of his shoes in each hand, looking at him. "You must believe in progress, at least for yourself."

"In a relative way. I'll never be somebody else, of course, though that's what I once wished for. But at least within myself I have changed, grown stronger, become more lucid. My revolt has paid off; you can see that; not completely, of course, I don't suppose that's ever possible; but look at me, chipper as a jaybird, comparatively speaking. That's something."

"A great deal. But aside from your subjective knowledge, are there any objective indications of the change?"

"Good Lord, yes. Hundreds. I notice new ones every day, most of them too shameful to bear talking about. But . . . well, my hands, for instance: they no longer tremble, except occasionally."

"Then you're no longer an aspen."

"Oh, I'm an aspen all right." He sniffed. "Maybe it's only winter and I've lost my leaves, maybe the wind has died down, momentarily."

"Never mind, aspens are beautiful at any time." She placed the shoes together, toes out, under the foot of the bed, army style. "Tell me really, how much have I had to do with your change?"

"It's hard to say," he answered slowly. "Yet I see what you mean: it's important, isn't it, after the recent discussions? Important to us. Certainly I made a start by myself; long, long ago, in fact. Impossible to say how long; the beginning was made when I wasn't aware of it. Painting was the big factor then, working things out on canvas, working intuitively with the images of my own feeling. Slowly a sort of organization emerged. And then Camus came to help, at first only through his books, the way they reaffirmed parts of my own experience, and I couldn't have managed as well as I did without him. Perhaps I couldn't have managed at all. Then you came. As if you were a prize, or a reward for what I'd done; and that's not a bad way to look at it. But it isn't the whole story, I'm certain, because I've done so marvelously . . . since the night you came to my room. Far better than before. If you had come sooner, the change would have been quicker. If you had come, somehow, to that other room . . ."

"I'm sorry I couldn't." She sat on a low stool by the hearth. "What about this?" she asked, tapping his plaster leg.

Aspen grinned. "You know, it's a case in point, a damned good one. I've done reasonably well, you'll admit, and in circumstances that would have been totally impossible a few months ago. My God, a hospital, a city! And I got out of it with no more than a bit of hysteria, maybe no more than anyone would have felt. Just a little moment of fragmentation. My revolt worked splendidly, in other words. Even in that frightful operating room. And it was a genuine revolt because it was conducted against a genuine absurdity and by means of a genuine lucidity. It was my own assininity that did it, after all, and that's the absurdity I know best. Camus and I differ most radically on just this point, I suppose; for him the manifestations of absurdity usually come from without, for me they come from within. He might say the absurdity was that wretched juniper growing too close to the path, while I say it was the jughead who put on the skis to begin with. However, that's not the point. The point is that I've asserted myself against it with a certain decorum and conviction; successfully, in other words. But alone? Without you? Impossible; I'd have gone to pieces."

"Why? What did I do?"

"That's just it, you didn't *do* anything. I mean I could have hired a nurse and someone to drive the Alfa. And yet I couldn't have managed without you, you yourself, simply because you *were*, you existed; the woman I love, the woman who loves me. You were a part of the revolt."

"How?"

"Let's say Camus hasn't told us quite everything about revolt. He says an act of revolt requires lucidity, but perhaps it requires lucidity plus something else: strength. After all, an act is only an act because it expresses force, isn't that so? Well, many people may possess within themselves the strength they need to revolt successfully; but obviously many other people do not, I'd say most other people. They must draw strength from without, sometimes from a totally abstract source, such as a political or religious idea, and sometimes from a less abstract but still generalized concept, such as the idea of compassion on which Camus relies so heavily. But for me the exterior source of strength must be something much more particular; it must be a fellowship which is intimate and personal and responsive. In the nature of things, this means a sexual fellowship."

"But how does it work?"

"You mean psychologically speaking? I don't know. Anyway, what difference does it make? We know it does work, why be metaphysical about it? If two people can say to one another, 'Look, we're in this together,' they both feel stronger. I suppose it's because none of us wants to suffer uniquely; that would be more absurdity than anyone could bear."

"Then why doesn't it last?"

"And why are you such a pessimist?" Aspen grimaced. "Of course, it does last, in one sense; it's as old as life, or at any rate as old as the records of the human mind and heart: sexual fellowship, with the emphasis equally on both terms. What you mean is why doesn't a particular love relationship last? Countless reasons, I suppose; there always are whenever two people break up. People being what they are, namely, absurd, I suppose one can't expect anything else. Yet the fact is we do expect something else at least some of the time, and our expectations are fulfilled. If absurdity bears against love as against life, then a marriage which is a self-sustaining revolt will be a self-sustaining marriage. Q.E.D." Aspen's tone softened. "I think we can do it, you and I. Call me a sentimentalist if you wish, but I'm being rational now, as much as anyone can. We have a certain toughness; you have always had it, I think, and I'm learning it now, too; and we are realists, even to the extent of 'realizing' that 'realism' admits and welcomes love. We are true rebels, and in consequence we and our love will change as the circumstances of our absurdity change; but that doesn't necessarily mean an end. On the contrary, since we are true rebels, it means permanence, such permanence as human beings can have. Relationships grow, just like individuals. I'll tell you what I think: if anything does us in, it will be the inequality of our love, I taking so much help from you without a chance to give help in return."

Dora studied her hands. "You think you haven't helped me?"

"I don't see how."

"You're wrong."

"Am I? Curiously, I'd be delighted if I were. But you seem so strong, as if you had always been strong, right from the beginning, as if your rebellion had always been intent, lucid, secure, in a sense achieved, as far as any rebellion is ever achieved, long before I met you. What can I have contributed? The change in me is obvious but what is the change in you?"

"My profession."

⊓⊔⊓⊔⊓

THEY ARRIVED back at the cliff house on 29 December. D'Arrast was already there; upon learning of Aspen's mishap, he became extremely solicitous, installed a comfortable chaise in the room with the blue and white floor, prepared broths and cutlets for Aspen's meals, and in general set himself up as nurse and factotum, until Aspen was visibly embarrassed. The sky was overcast; but the chill of winter remained in the air. Veils of mist stirred heavily in the cold breeze, and the windows were beaded with moisture. Finally, when D'Arrast asked for the hundreth time if there was something he could do, Aspen said: "Yes, you can pose for me," and for a day Aspen did sketches of the burly *Algérien* dressed in a cap and seaman's jacket. Afterward, he came to regard these sketches as among the best of his work.

Camus rejoined them on New Year's Eve. They had a splendid dinner, cooked by D'Arrast with Dora's assistance, of cold *morue*, a dish of curried pigeons, a ham cooked in the American manner, and a dessert of *crème à Moravie*. Camus supplied champagne, and Aspen had sent Dora, early in the day, to buy fruit, nuts, chocolates, cognac, and candles. The dining table was set in the large room, so that Aspen's chaise could be drawn alongside. Everyone was in a good mood.

When the time came for toasts, D'Arrast said simply: "Let's drink to the new year: may it be a good one for us all."

After they set down their goblets, Camus said: "You know, I believe it will be, too. A good year. I have a lucky feeling."

"Change of mood?" D'Arrast asked.

"Yes."

"Good," Aspen said. "And appropriate. I've a lucky feeling myself, if it comes to that, and with good reason. I'm the only one here who can say with virtual certainty that the next year will be better for me than the last. Thanks largely to you."

"To me?" Camus seemed genuinely surprised.

"Of course. I wouldn't be here if it hadn't been for you."

"You'd have come to the same thing, or practically, on your own."

"That's hard to believe. Aside from your bringing me to this house, don't you grant any communicative powers at all to your novels, any social efficacy? Do you write them solely for yourself?"

"No, of course not. Or rather, why I write them is my own affair, but obviously I publish them for other people. But let's not start a discussion tonight, shall we? Thinking is death, and this isn't the time for it."

"As you wish, of course. Though, for that matter, what else have we to talk about? And I must say that's a rather peculiar statement to hear from someone who has always seemed proud to be an intellectual."

"That thinking is death?"

"Yes. Did you mean it?"

"In a manner of speaking. And I see no reason why an intellectual should be embarrassed by his concern for death. On the contrary, it is an honorable burden; even an altruistic burden."

"How do you mean that thinking is death?" D'Arrast put in.

"Nothing particularly novel. Simply that death is the source of thought, the goad, the incitement. Without death, thinking would never have been required. Isn't it a truism that what distinguishes us from the animals is our self-awareness of death? Then in a manner of speaking all thought is ultimately reduced, or rather condensed, consolidated, crystallized, to the idea of death."

"We presume you are speaking as an artist," Aspen remarked.

"I always must, naturally. But what do you mean in this instance?"

"That your statement would be vigorously disputed by a good many people who believe that their thought is stimulated by very different considerations. Curiosity, for example; or economic necessity. But if you intend your statement to serve as a radical conceptualization, a structure of imagination, a touchstone, or whatever you wish to call it, perhaps almost a symbol in the broadest and most dynamic application of the term; in other words, if you offer your statement as a work of art, not as a work of analysis or ratiocination, then I'd say that for me it is perfectly justifiable and, moreover, damned useful."

"But of course. That is the only kind of statement I could possibly make, the only kind that exists. Haven't we said that that 'logical' thought is a fiction?"

"Yes, we have said it, you have written it; but it is a point that needs reinforcing from time to time, I think, because we slip back into our old habits so easily. It's an important point for me; if I've learned anything these past six months, it is that the imagination can serve me well, the conceptualizing imagination. Not simply as an artist, but as a proper philosopher, a seeker of practical wisdom. My imagination can give me, has given me, a systematic view of reality, which is pretty extraordinary in itself, but the main thing is that it works, it really and truly works. I can live by it."

"But is it the truth, objectively speaking?" D'Arrast asked.

"Yes, that's precisely what would have hung me up like a plucked chicken a few months ago. But now I just say, 'Who cares?' Your question goes into the system, so to speak: truth is absurd, truth is the unknowable. Consequently, it is what we confront; it is what we oppose and exclude. Not so difficult, really, once you get the hang of it."

"It works?" Camus asked.

"Yes, for me, now. I don't say one can stand still in it. In fact, the whole point of it is that one can't. And I think we must acknowledge a greater flexibility than I had been thinking of in the past. If what we know is composed, not of truth, but of fact, then our knowledge must change as we acquire more facts. This is obvious, but what people do not take sufficiently into account is the degree to which it forces fluidity upon us. Our rebellion is continually changing; our imaginations are continually active. For instance, against your statement that thinking is death I would place another: that living is love. But I'm not sure the rest of you would agree with it."

There was a period of silence. Then Camus said: "Do you, D'Arrast?"

"Yes, I think so."

"And you?"

"Yes," Dora said.

"Then I find myself in a minority, as usual." Camus smiled. "I'm not sure I can accept Aspen's statement altogether. I'm not sure I see the same complete crystallization in respect to loving and life that I see in respect to thinking and death. But it's neat, I grant you; it has the inclusiveness of a work of art, provided you can enforce it. That's the trouble with works of art: they aren't machines; they won't run by themselves; you have to make them run."

"Was that Meursault's trouble?" D'Arrast asked. "That he was a poor artist?"

"Yes, I was waiting for that guy to show up. The evening wouldn't be complete without him, would it? And what a fellow he must have been, to haunt us so persistently. All right, let's put him to a final scrutiny. Certainly he lacked imagination; I'd say that is as close as we can come to a final statement of his defect: he suffered from a virtually total imaginative sclerosis. But that isn't the same as saying he should have been an artist. On the contrary, if he had been simply an artist, if he had suffered, let us say, from an imaginative hypertrophy, he might not have done anything at all." Camus pushed back his chair from the table, and crossed his legs. "Meursault ran aground when he committed an act of revolt which was misdirected and wrong. It follows, then, that what he should have been, primarily, was a good rebel, not an artist or anything else. Mind you, I happen to believe that an artist, if he is worth his salt, will almost always be a good rebel; he has a headstart, so to speak, over other people. But that doesn't mean other people may not be good rebels, too, if they understand the nature of revolt."

"Have you found a way out of your corner?" Dora asked.

Camus smiled again. "It isn't as simple as that, Dora. But I think I see a glimmer. As a matter of fact, I have seen it for some time, but I haven't known precisely what to do with it, and certain problems have arisen; though, as far as that goes, it's fundamentally simple enough." He took a cigarette from a pack on the table and lighted it. "First, however, let's go back, incidentally, to a remark of Aspen's a moment ago, when he spoke of the flexibility of revolt. It's an important point, I think. Hasn't a great deal of our discussion so far been an attempt to impose form on content, to say that an act of revolt must have this or that shape? But the fact is that it may take any shape, and the choice is an individual matter. One may revolt in terms of art or love or work or commerce or whatever; possibly, if one believes, one may revolt even in terms of religion, although that's a tricky point. What makes the revolt genuine is not its form but its objective, its passion, and its lucidity; and these are the terms upon which we must insist.

"These terms, you see, are not an individual matter, they apply to all revolt, to the universal substance of revolt. But the very individuality of mere form, mere style, is what leads us into our difficulty.

"Let me recapitulate. The act of revolt by its very nature extends beyond the individual person. The individual revolt is an assertion of an individual claim to the integrity of an individual life, but it can legitimate itself only by acknowledging the same claim made by everyone else in the world. Thus an act of revolt which endangers the integrity of another person's life invalidates itself. But since any act of revolt, any assertion of an individual claim, raises precisely this danger, revolt itself becomes illegitimate. Thus revolt contains its own invalidation. And this was what led me, very reluctantly, to retreat into the concept of art-as-revolt.

"It was a mistake. A work of art asserts no claim but the artist's. I don't see any way out of that, because I don't see any

way to presume a necessary causal link between the work of
art and anyone else. Such a causal link may spring up, of course;
literature is simply a complex of such relationships. But they
aren't necessary. They are fortuitous only, however well they
may conform to a causal mode of operation once they are in
existence. I repeat, the work of art asserts only the artist's claim,
without any necessary acknowledgment of the claim of others.
In consequence, it cannot be a revolt."

"Isn't it possible that a work of art can be both a work of
art and a revolt?" Aspen said.

"Yes, but let's not get into that now, it's too involved in
distinctions. I am speaking of the work of art as a work of art:
an autotelic esthetic object. As such, it cannot be considered
an act of revolt. Which leaves us . . . where? Rather up in
the air, it seems. We have no choice, I take it, but to return
to fundamentals, to work back into the question of revolt itself,
and I should say a good place to begin is by asking simply:
what is a rebel?

"Let's not be academic about it; good heavens, we know
what a rebel is. Yet we have talked him practically out of existence. He is a . . . a rebel, no? Someone who kicks over the
traces, to put it mildly. A person who opposes the constraints
pressing upon his own existence, a person *who acts in terms of
the world*. And what is the nature of his act?" Camus paused.
Then: "It's a denial, a denial; that's what we had lost sight of,
though we had it firmly enough in mind at the beginning.
And a denial does not interdict the justifiable claims of another
person. Do you remember the distinction we made between
rights and privileges? Well, look at it this way: if I deny the
constraints imposed upon me, I oppose the other person only
to the extent that his *privilege* contravenes my claim to existence, I do not destroy the *right* of the other person's claim to
his own existence. It was Meursault's duty to deny the privilege
of absurdity, but not to deny the right of the Arab. And let's
not make the mistake of thinking that denial, simply because

it is a negation, is therefore not an act; on the contrary, it is an assertion in the full sense, an act in terms of the world. We have seen this how many thousands of times in our own lives, here in this unhappy Europe?

"To sum up. Revolt in its fundamental nature is denial, and denial fulfills all the requirements of our definition of revolt: it is an act, it asserts the claim of the individual person, it acknowledges the claims of other persons, and it becomes a full revolt when it is committed in passion and lucidity."

"Is it . . . nonviolence?"

"Gandhi's philosophy. I have been thinking about him a great deal lately. I think he must have been the only saint our century has produced. Frankly, I could give myself to his teaching with the utmost satisfaction. Before his accomplishments, his spirit, one may only admire and praise. And yet something, a tiny distinction, holds me back. *Ahimsa* is, after all, a product of a particular civilization; a magnificent product, a flowering of Indian thought and feeling so beautiful and so filled with humane passion that it is one of the cresting movements of all being; the generations that come after us may look upon our European perplexities at this moment as fumblings in the outer darkness. We are a little like the outlanders at the time of Christ who could only look on with longing, recognizing that a thousand considerations of locality and cultural dispersion disqualified them from any closer concurrence. For the fact is that Indian civilization has not arrived at the view of absurdity which we Europeans hold inescapably. And we cannot give it up, any more than we can change the color of our skins. Absurdity is what we are, what we, the Europeans of the twentieth century, have been born into; it is as much a part of our existence as our diet.

"Then it comes to this: self-defense. Legitimate or not? For us it must be, I see no other way; because self-defense is simply a name for denial, and denial is simply a name for revolt. It places the emphasis somewhat differently from our custom heretofore, no doubt, and I myself wouldn't normally use the term. But there it is; one has the right to defend one's claim, and in some cases this means violence. Not often, certainly not as often as people think; but the extreme case remains a possibility. I am forced to revert to my original concept of denial, an assertion of one's claim only to the extent that the claim is defended, without permitting the claim to become an assertion of privilege. I add only that if this requires violence, the violence must end at the very instant when the defense has been made."

"And in practice . . ."

"And in practice this may mean the deprivation of another's life, if the other insists on exerting his privilege to the point of an ultimate confrontation. I acknowledge the possibility. What is one to do? One cannot permit oneself to be exterminated, that is fundamental; nor can one, finally, run away, since privilege will always pursue. In this extremity, I consider that the fault lies with the oppressor entirely. Mind you, I say I shall do no murder, none whatever, and I do not consider that I have moved a jot from this position; I still deny, as a matter of principle, every ground on which the state presumes to take the life of an individual person, because the state has no right at all; it is complete privilege; and I still deny every aggressive attack on life, since this is plainly inimical to genuine revolt. One's assertion must be made only against a clear and immediate constraint. Granted, it isn't easy to decide, often enough, when a constraint is clear and immediate, and that is perhaps one of the principal attractions of nonviolence, taken as an ideal, an absolute rule of conduct: it removes the necessity of deciding. But ultimately I think one cannot avoid deciding, if one is to make a genuine revolt; that is the human lot, and in a very proper sense the decision is part of the revolt." Camus paused, and raised his cognac to his lips, setting it down again, however, without sipping. "Yes, one must decide. And when others are clearly and immediately exposed to the absurdity of deprived selfhood, when they attempt, through their denial, a genuine act of revolt, then one must decide, too; with caution, no doubt, with attention to conflicting claims, but . . . one can't put it off forever."

"In Algeria?"

"Yes, in Algeria."

⎍⎍⎍⎍

FOR SEVERAL days Camus worked, more or less diligently, keeping to his room in the mornings and occasionally hurrying off during afternoons and evenings to scribble down something he wished to remember. From time to time the sound of his portable typewriter was heard. He made a cheerful appearance, joked a good deal with Aspen and D'Arrast, and kidded Dora, who was inclined to be too somber; but sometimes he plainly wasn't listening when the others spoke. On the fourth morning his typewriter mumbled uninterruptedly behind his door for some time, and then stopped. When Camus appeared for lunch, he sat down heavily.

"How does it go?" D'Arrast said.

"Basically, okay. But I'm not happy about parts; it's the devil's own job to make the actual position take root in particular circumstances."

"As we have seen," Aspen said.

"It will have to sit for a while, I'm afraid, then maybe it will grow. But don't fret, I'll be in touch with you from Paris."

"Still planning to leave tomorrow?"

"Yes, this interlude has come to an end, hasn't it?"

No one said anything, and Aspen nodded as if to himself, expressing mingled satisfaction and regret.

"Going by train?" D'Arrast said finally.

Camus answered yes, and added, with a smile: "Since Aspen has a new passenger."

D'Arrast said: "It's Aspen who'll be the passenger, at least for a while." Then to Aspen: "How does it feel today?"

"Fine. I'll be out of the cast in no time."

"Don't rush it. Do you know who your doctor will be?"

"No. But those Swiss sawbones ought to be first-class when it comes to ski accidents. I'm not worried."

"Sawbones?"

"Doctors." Aspen looked down at his plate. "Is it indiscreet to ask your plans?"

"I'm afraid it is," D'Arrast said, and the conversation turned to other matters.

ᒪᒪᒪᒪᒐ

THAT EVENING, Aspen said: "Still and all, now that it has been done, I suppose I must confess I'm sorry, in a way, to have heard you depreciate the role of the artist."

"I know what you mean, of course. Nostalgia extends its appeals at every turn, no less for the most recent of the mind's yearnings than for the most ancient. Who couldn't wish to succumb? The word itself, nostalgia, is like soft music over the water, sunny and African." Camus rubbed the back of his left hand with the palm of his right. "Nevertheless, it is depreciation in the technical sense alone. We artists needn't despair, we have our pride, our justification; in two ways, as a matter of fact: first, the pride of our self-denying intellect, which musters the rather considerable courage needed to reject nostalgia, and second, the pride of our undiminishable grandeur. For if we must discriminate technically, in order to safeguard our premises and our honesty, between the rebel and the artist, according the former the more intrinsically human role, we know that the latter furnishes our only enduring examples. Art is concrete; it is all we have on our side, ultimately, that is concrete. Its purity, its candor and restlessness, its firmness, its beauty, these are our only enduring counterbalances to the filth and depravity of an absurd existence. If art itself is not an act, in the important overreaching sense we have ascribed to the term, then it nevertheless may inspire an act, and often it does; fully often enough to permit us to retain our artistic faith. Aside from our other benefactions of beauty and intelligence, which in private we may assert without immodesty, we cultivate, as artists, history's only humane talent; and hence we are the readiest to become rebels, and the most skillful in revolt. Nothing has ever been done which was not first suggested by us. We have a frightening but a beautiful authority, and we are the only ones in a lonely universe with the wisdom to exercise it. We are the princes of lucidity."

⎍⎍⎍⎍

LATER, D'ARRAST took his leave. He shook hands all around, saying: "I'll delegate the locking up to you. Put the key on the ledge over the door, someone will come for it later. Good-bye." And he walked away swiftly into the darkness, carrying a brown canvas bag in his left hand.

Camus stood looking into the night. "We have no heroes in our age; everyone knows that; a preposterous, old-fashioned idea. But I think I . . ." He stopped and frowned, put a cigarette in his lips, began to say something but stopped again, and turned and walked out of the room.

⌐⊓⌐⊓⌐⊓

AS IT turned out, Camus caught a ride, at the last minute, with a friend from Paris, who drove up the next morning in a Facel Vega HK-500. Introductions were performed, and Aspen asked immediately if he might look under the hood. "A V-8," he murmured. "Powerful plant for a smallish vehicle. What's the displacement?"

"Trifle over 5000 cc's."

"Bhp?"

"Rated about 360 at 5200 rpm."

"Mmmmm. Acceleration?"

"Zero to a hundred in 20 seconds."

"You could drive a ship with it."

"You could."

"Suspension?"

"Coils in front, semi-elliptics behind."

"Bit stiff, eh?"

"That's the hitch, of course. She's rocky on the turns, you have to be careful. But the power makes up for it."

"Mmmmmmmm."

Luggage was stowed quickly in the two cars, and they walked through the empty house, looking for things they might have forgotten. It was cold, and their voices rang in the brittle air. Dora was carrying Aspen's stone. "He wanted to leave it behind," she said to Camus, "but I thought . . ." She shrugged, smiling gravely. Aspen sniffed.

Ten minutes later, they took off, the Facel Vega showing the way, the Alfa following. It was a gray morning, threatening rain. The Facel Vega flew, sinking noticeably as it accelerated on the straights, but Dora managed to keep in sight.

Near Valence the route forked. The Facel Vega slowed, but did not stop, on the otherwise empty highway. Dora and Aspen caught a glimpse of Camus at the car window, his face half-obscured by his hatbrim and the collar of his trench coat. There was a wave of a hand. Then the Facel Vega accelerated and sped to the north, while the Alfa turned toward the east, moving at a more moderate but adequate speed.

THE END

Author's Note

No doubt the reasons for the somewhat unusual form of this book are so obscurely embedded in my own temperament that it would be unprofitable to try speaking of them. One superficial reason was my feeling that the five or six books of conventional exegesis already devoted to Camus in English are enough for the time being. Beyond that, my wish was to combine homage with inquiry, and I can say only that the form of my endeavor proceeded quite naturally from my intention.

Probably some readers will be offended by the way I have used Albert Camus as a fiction, not to say a fantasy. I apologize to them, and assure them my purpose was nothing reprehensible. To other readers, who may be unsuspecting, I will say expressly that in writing about the person called "Camus" in this book I have intended only the sketchiest possible reference to the biography of the actual Camus. At the same time, however, I hope my invention is at least roughly consistent with the character of the actual man as we see it in his writing. If I have put words, many thousands of words, into the mouth of Camus, they take a direction which I, in my respect and admiration, believe he would have taken if he had found himself in the circumstances I have imagined. But of course he would have spoken more clearly and cogently.

In short, this is a venture in extreme speculation. I have tried to attribute to Camus nothing, either in mood or substance, which cannot be inferred or justly extrapolated from his own books, but in such an attempt success is out of the question. The most I can think is that what I have done is perhaps suggestive and arguable.

I apologize also for the repetitions which the narrative seemed to require, and for the lack of scholarly method. Over the years my interest in Camus has been personal and pragmatic; hence it is not possible to list all the works I have consulted, some systematically but others desultorily. I shall limit myself to saying that I have been especially helped by John Cruickshank's *Albert Camus and the Literature of Revolt* (Oxford University Press, 1959) and by Lawrence Goldman's fine essay in the second number of the quarterly *Root and Branch* (undated; Berkeley, California). And I have three additional acknowledgments: to my friend Wallace Fowlie for help with a question of language, to Edouard Morot-Sir of the French Cultural Service for help with a question of fact, and to the Bollingen Foundation for a fellowship which enabled me to write this book. My debt to the trustees and officers of the foundation is great indeed.

Albert Camus was deeply, even fiercely committed to his work and his beliefs, yet he was never afraid to run the risk of undeception. I have tried to follow him. "We have a right to think," he wrote a year or two before he died, "that truth with a capital letter is relative. But facts are facts. And whoever says that the sky is blue when it is gray is prostituting words and preparing the way for tyranny."

H.C.

December 20, 1963